Book Three of Luna's Story
DIANA KNIGHTLEY

Other titles by Diana Knightley can be found here:

Leveling: Book One of Luna's Story

Under: Book Two of Luna's Story

Deep: Book Three of Luna's Story

Diana Knightley.com

For Isobel, Fiona, Gwyneth, and Ean
Keep your chin up.

Part One:

The Road

Chapter 1

Beckett stood in a hallway of the temporary bunk-house with his release forms in his hands. His duty was officially over. Six years done. The past six months of fighting in the East, over. He was done with bombs and shrapnel and explosions and near misses. For good. He had survived. It had gone faster than he thought it would, like he had been in a trance and was waking up now, still alive.

Now he got to go home. The paperwork said so. His name was written across the top. It said in bold face: Released from Duty. It bore today's date.

There was a big problem though. He had to get home.

He thought there'd be a bus, but apparently those only go one way or some other kind of bullshit. The officer that passed Beckett the paperwork seemed to think it was beneath his station to also arrange for Beckett's ride home. The trains were stopped because of skirmishes around the tracks. The airport was north through heavily bombed areas, a no-man's-land.

Beckett had been told to sit tight and wait for a ride.

When he asked how long it might take the answer was, "Weeks, if you're lucky."

He banged the back of his head against the wall. "Damn."

He went to the mess hall for lunch — one table, three guys, a basket with "provisions." Beckett chose the bar that tasted, if you had a good enough imagination, like bacon.

Turk asked, "Homeward bound?"

Beckett slammed the paperwork on the table and shook his head.

"Ah, you my friend, have entered the seventh level of hell. Welcome."

"I thought you were injured?"

"I am." Turk patted the side of his immobile leg. "Bad enough to get me a ticket home, just no transport. I'm waiting in this bunk, praying it doesn't explode before I get to leave. If you think about it, it's one big cosmic fucking joke. The kind that makes you laugh 'til you cry."

"My job was to protect the rail lines and the ports. I guess I should have protected harder because they don't work."

"No supplies either. Munitions though, seems those shipments always get through."

Beckett ripped open the top of the bar and took a big devouring bite. "If I was an arms dealer I could get through." The windows rattled with a faraway explosion.

Turk ducked. "If you were an arms dealer, you wouldn't get to go home, so yeah, that's not the best plan. You got a home to go back to?"

"I do. And a girl."

"Phewee, this is gonna be a tough wait for you then. Me, I'm sitting because I can't walk, can't do anything but wait. You got two legs. You have to wait and hope they don't," he used his fingers to add quotations around, "sign you back up."

Beckett clenched his teeth. "They could sign me back up?"

"They have the enemy at the gates, fucking assholes, and all those body bags to fill." Turk chuckled. "If I were you I'd look busy."

Beckett said, "I could walk out. West."

"That you could, and you're a free man. I'd go with you if I could. Take food and water, stay clear of the military roads. It'd be three days before you get to a civilian road. With all the refugee movement you're sure to get a ride with someone." Turk stood and pulled crutches to his side, wobbling as he balanced. "And Beckett, a bit of advice. You'll want to keep the bombs behind you, if they're in front of you you're going the wrong way."

He turned and lurched to the door. "Hope I don't see you tomorrow."

"Yeah Turk, you too." Beckett finished his breakfast, ran his hands over the bristle on his head, put his elbows on the table resting his mouth on his fists. He glanced around the room. He could fill a bag with food. Take his hydration pack. He would really need his helmet and a gun, but that was Mainland property. He couldn't risk the trouble; he'd have to go without.

He would take some food, water, and his personal things. And go. That's all he needed to do.

There were maps hanging on the wall, old, antiquated. He located his base on one and followed his finger down a trail to a highway. It would take about three days through the woods. South then west. He took a photo of the map and gathered his things.

Chapter 2

Six months had passed.

Luna's eyes opened. She glanced around her small room. The light was dim — raining. She shifted all the pillows she slept around and on, flipped the quilt off, and jumped up. She had slept in a simple pair of underwear, tight now that she had curves in every direction. Her stomach protruded, round and tight. Her belly button poked out. Stretch marks spread from her waist down her hips. She tugged on a small t-shirt that stretched over the top of her belly and pulled on a pair of pajama pants Dilly had given her. And tied them under her belly. She ran fingers through her hair and raced to the kitchen. "Did he come yet?"

"No dearest, not yet." Chickadee checked her watch. "Even with the best of intentions, with no setbacks, he still has to ride home. That's three hours. so he can't possibly get here before ten."

Dilly set a cup of coffee in front of Luna. "That's if he was still stationed on the coast, and you know I've had my doubts, I'm guessing at least six hours."

Luna poured milk in the mug and stirred it briskly. "But you've both been up for hours."

"I've been waiting since five-thirty," Chickadee said. "I'm too excited to sleep."

"Plus she was too excited to let me sleep." Dilly dropped into a chair and smiled at Luna.

Luna smiled back.

Chickadee beamed at them both.

They in unison raised their mugs to their lips.

Chickadee laughed. "So is this what we're going to do, stare at each other until he gets home?"

"Nope, we need to get busy," said Dilly. "A project. Um—"

"Spring cleaning!" Chickadee disappeared into the laundry room, returning with spray and a stack of towels. "We'll wash every window. Inside, since it's raining outside. It will be symbolic since we're watching for him. Before we blink twice, he'll be walking up the driveway." She plopped the supplies on the table. "After breakfast of course."

The three of them washed all the windows. They stripped the beds and vacuumed all the floors. At ten o'clock Dilly went to the market for ingredients for Beckett's homecoming meal. Leaving, she procured a promise if Beckett arrived while she was gone they would convince him to come home a second time so she could experience it too. At one o'clock they ate sandwiches on the porch watching the rain continue to pour.

Chickadee said, "Any minute now."

In the afternoon Luna un-cobwebbed the house, while Chickadee answered some of her business mail, and Dilly laundered the sheets. Around three Luna resorted to leaning over the back of the couch watching out the front living room window. After a little while Dilly leaned beside her.

Luna asked, "Do you think we have the right day?"

"It's the day he told us, months ago. I have it on the calendar."

Luna went to look at the calendar for the tenth time that day. Chickadee said, as she walked past, "I just checked it, the date hasn't changed."

"I know, I just have to look."

The calendar had a scrawled note in red ink and circled four times: Beckett comes home!!!

Luna returned to the couch.

Dilly said, "Any minute now."

Around four o'clock, Roscoe called to check if Beckett was home. Then Chickadee's friend Peter called, and her friend Tina. Luna and Dilly decided to dust all the books.

Around five o'clock they decided to organize the books according to color. It took a while to map out which color to start with. They had to compensate for the fact that all the tall books were darker, but there were a lot more white books. The project was satisfying, and Luna kept working on it while Dilly made the welcome home dinner, coming in now and then to say, "Brilliant!" and "Perfect!"

Chickadee came in when they were about halfway done, hands on her hips. "Hmm, not so sure."

Luna faltered in the middle of placing blue books on the blue shelf.

Dilly said, "But look how pretty!"

Chickadee humphed. "Aren't books supposed to be educational and interesting, and aren't we supposed to be above judging them by their cover and making rainbows with their bindings?"

Dilly said, "That is all true, but I'll say it again, look how pretty!"

"Yes, it's pretty. Still feels wrong, but then again — " Chickadee stalked to the front door and whisked it open and stared out into the rain. "Where's that boy?"

"Exactly," said Dilly. "When Luna and I get done arranging the books in this rainbow, we'll all look at them, Beckett included, and we'll vote. If the rainbow sucks, Luna will put them back. Right Luna?"

"I'll do whatever I need to to get my mind off this — have you tried calling again?"

Chickadee said, "I just did. Again. Still no answer, same as it was for the last ten weeks. Just a clicking noise. But he said there would be no contact. He told us to sit tight. He would be released on this date, and he'd see us, and I haven't heard . . ." Her voice trailed off, she twisted the necklace resting on her chest.

Dilly paused for a moment and then handed Luna three books. "Aqua blue, I think those go over there."

———————————

At eight o'clock they ate dinner without Beckett. The rain was still pouring down.

———————————

At ten they headed to bed.

Sometime in the middle of the night Luna finally fell asleep.

Chapter 3

Luna slept longer than she intended. Of course, if Beckett was there — or if he had called — she would have been told, but she rushed into the kitchen anyway, hopeful and excited.

Then she saw the faces of Dilly and Chickadee, and her heart fell into her shoes.

Dilly spoke immediately, nervously. "If you think about it, we didn't actually know he would come home the first day. He probably needed to finish up paperwork, get his clearance, arrange for transport home."

Luna stood and nodded dumbly.

"Yes, well, and exactly," said Chickadee. "But since he's not answering his blasted phone, I need to figure out what time he's coming home because my heart can't take eating another of his favorite meals without him here to share it." She grabbed her keys and headed for the door.

Dilly asked, "Where are you going, it's pouring outside!"

"I plan to go talk to Roscoe and maybe go ask at the market. I also think I should check with Dryden's family—" She held up her hands even though no one protested against the idea. "Just in case he's been in touch with them — my apologies Luna"

Luna chewed her lip. "You're right. You should ask. Of course."

Chickadee gave her a small sad smile. "I'll be back in a few hours, Dearest." She paused at the door. "Call me, if he shows."

Dilly nodded.

Chickadee slammed the door as she left.

"What if . . ." Luna's voice trailed off, but her eyes were frightened.

And Dilly was too upset to allow for it.

"What if Dryden's heard from him? Well we'll have to cross that bridge—"

"Yes. Right." Luna poured more coffee into her mug, thinking, that wasn't really the scariest What-If. Her What-If was bigger, scarier, impossible to speak. What if something had happened to Beckett, would they know? How would they know? And oh god, what if they were waiting and he — he — what *if?*

She slumped into a yellow kitchen chair and commenced to waiting for word while Dilly puttered nervously around the kitchen.

At two in the afternoon, Chickadee's car rumbled up the drive, and then, soaked, Chickadee slammed through the front door dripping all over the rug. "I have Roscoe looking for him. So that's good. Dryden's mother said they hadn't spoken in months, but on further pressing, she realized it had been over a year. None of his old buddies knew anything. So yeah. And Dilly, there's something in the car for you." She was flustered and breathing heavy as she dropped her raincoat to the floor.

Dilly looked incredulous. "Something for me — in the car? You want me to go out in the rain for it?"

"Well you can't wait. It will chew through the goddamned seat."

Dilly's eyes went wide. "It's an animal?"

Chickadee sighed. "They had puppies at the freaking market, and I was so distracted with worry somehow I managed to take one home with me. Now you'll have to love it or I'm the worst person in the world."

"A puppy!" Dilly shoved her arms into her raincoat's sleeves.

Chickadee dropped into a chair. "Oh Luna, dear Luna, I wish I had better news for you."

"Well, you tried. And if you think about it Beckett could walk in here any minute."

Dilly returned from the car, squealing, "Oh my god, do you see this Luna?"

She held up a small golden-colored puppy. Looking into its eyes she said, "You are so adorable. Oh, I am going to love you, and you'll have to be wonderful, not like that last dog, better than that, in every way. Won't you little guy?"

She turned to Luna, "We'll spend the afternoon waiting for Beckett and coming up with a name for this puppy." She screwed up her face and rubbed it on her cheek pretending to cry. "I already love it so much!"

Luna chuckled, the closest thing to happy she had felt in hours. But it only lasted for a moment. Chickadee pulled her phone from her pocket, dropped it to the table, and menacing toward it, said, "Ring, dammit."

Chapter 4

Beckett trudged through the forest.

In retrospect it seemed like the dumbest thing in the world to leave base and go like this. The only person who knew he was gone was Turk. He should have left a note because the worst part? He had been walking for about twelve hours over two days and still had no phone service.

He guessed he was headed in the right direction. He was pretty good at such things, not a navigator, but good enough. But here was the thing, rain was coming. Lots of rain. He would need to hunker down. He had a rain coat, but this was a full blown storm. Crap, this water wouldn't ever fucking stop.

He walked for another hour then found a patch of underbrush that was higher than the path and covered by dense foliage. He climbed under it, wrapped his coat tightly around, and hunkered down, attempting to Go Bird, like Luna had said.

Chapter 5

Day three, Luna rose earlier and met Dilly in the kitchen where the puppy was going bonkers, biting every everything that moved, and alternately chewing on a sock she wasn't supposed to have.

Dilly kissed Luna on the cheek. "She whined a lot last night. She's lucky she's very cute."

Luna poured a cup of coffee for herself as Chickadee stormed in. "Nothing. A whole 'nother night passed." She slammed a mug down, poured four spoonfuls of sugar into it and filled it with coffee. "What the hell am I supposed to do with no information?" She was talking to the mug. "If I knew where he was I would go get him — that's what I'd do. By car or train or airplane—" She kissed Dilly on the cheek. "Did you sleep any better?"

Dilly pulled the puppy off the leg of her pajama pants. "Not at all."

They both turned to Luna who burst into tears. Because pregnant. Because hormonal. Because Beckett wasn't coming home.

Chickadee rushed across the kitchen, clucking. "Dear, dear, now don't you worry, aunt Chickadee was having a moment. This is all under control. You don't need to worry about anything. Beckie will be home any minute now." She scooped up the puppy and hugged Luna with the puppy in the middle of the huddle. The puppy chewed on Chickadee's earlobe.

Luna laughed through her tears.

"Dilly what have you named this little asshole?"

"Luna was thinking, Shark."

Luna sniffled, wiped her nose, and then fiddled nervously with the soggy wad of handkerchief. "Because it wants to bite you, but you can't hold it against him, because it's simply in his nature."

Chickadee held the puppy up and looked in its eyes. "I like it. There are an awful lot of terrifying things just acting out their nature, huh? I like it a lot. Okay, Shark, down you go, and leave my pajama pants alone. I'm round in the middle, so if you pull them down I've got no hips to slow their descent and you'll expose me to the whole world." The puppy sat and cocked her head at Chickadee. Chickadee said, "She gets me."

She turned to Luna. "How are you holding up?"

"Okay, I suppose . . ."

Chickadee said, "Yes, I agree, I feel the same way."

There was a strong bang on the screen door. Chickadee yelped, startled.

Roscoe's voice came from the porch. "Chickadee, I need to talk to you, I have some news about Beckett."

Chickadee's eyes went wide, terrified. "Oh no you don't Roscoe. Don't you come here with bad news. I won't — you call me." She collapsed into a chair. "If you're going to tell me something awful, you can't come in. I won't allow it. Oh, you're terrifying me, Roscoe. You can't—"

"Chickadee, it's not good, but it's not the worst either, let me in. I want to tell you in person."

Chickadee clutched the hem of Dilly's shirt. "I can't let him in. He's going to say something awful, and I don't want to know."

Dilly placed her mug on the counter, smoothed her hair, straightened her spine, and marched to the front door.

Chickadee stared in that direction. Unable to comfort Luna who stood quietly crying in the kitchen, unable to move or speak or anything as if she had gone frozen while the world spun and time moved in slow motion. Maybe that was a good thing — to freeze right there, before hearing whatever it was Roscoe had driven over at the crack of dawn to tell them.

Roscoe brushed past Dilly, entered the kitchen, and dropped into a chair opposite Chickadee. "Beckett is missing."

Chickadee's mouth moved silently repeating the word.

"He's been missing for going on three days."

"In action?"

"No Chickadee, he's been released from duty."

Dilly asked, "So he's on a bus home?"

"No, there's no record of him leaving in transportation. There's also no record of him on the base, at the front, or at meals. His commanding officer seemed to think that was all acceptable information."

Chickadee asked again, "Missing? From the base? What the hell?"

Dilly said, "It must be a paperwork issue."

"It would help greatly if we knew which base he had been stationed at." Luna was absentmindedly petting the puppy.

Chickadee pointed at her. "Exactly! What base?"

"This is also not good news. He's been at Burnside, at the front."

Chickadee ran her hands down her face. "At Burnside. Just this morning I saw a headline that said it was all fire, death, and destruction in Burnside, and that's where Beckett has been? That's where he is now, but there's no record of him?"

"Exactly."

Luna clenched her eyes and tight. "Did you check the hospitals?"

"There's also very little communication in and out."

Chickadee put her hand on Roscoe's. "I can't stay here waiting. I have to do something."

Roscoe said, "I know you do. I figured we'd start with battalion headquarters on the coast. I'll drive."

"Good, because I don't think I can concentrate." Chickadee hefted herself to standing. "Dilly, if Beckie calls, you call me the second you hear where he is."

"Of course, and you bring him home."

Chickadee turned to Luna. "Sweetie, I'm going to go get Beckie. You try not to worry, play with Shark. You have a baby you're growing and worry is . . ."

Luna nodded. "Yes, I'll try not to worry."

Roscoe and Chickadee hustled out the front door. A second later Chickadee burst back in. "I forgot to change out of my pajamas!"

She raced into the bedroom returning a couple minutes later and lovingly saying goodbye once more.

Chapter 6

The following day the rain stopped. Beckett trudged through the damp forest, closer now to the road. He would make it by the end of the day and then hitchhike home. Easy. Also, and most importantly, there would be phone service. He felt sure of it.

At about five o'clock he found the road. Trouble was, the lane west was full of cars, a parking lot of cars, trucks, vans as far as his eyes could see. Every vehicle was full of bundles and packages and luggage and people. People in every seat and piled in the back of trucks and even sitting up on top.

His phone was close to dead. He needed his solar panel to recharge but there hadn't been sun in days. And even though he knew to save the battery, he still kept turning it on to check for service, thinking, *maybe a call came through, a message, anything.* But no, he simply, idiotically, ran down the battery with all that checking.

He trudged up to the first car he came to, a man, a woman, three other people crammed in the back seat, and leaned into the window. "Excuse me, I'm looking for transportation west."

The man scoffed. "Like the rest of us." A truck whizzed by the other lane headed east. The driver asked, "Do you have any food?"

Beckett made a mental count of his bars: six. Not enough to bargain with, barely enough for himself now that his trip home looked so complicated. "I don't, but I'd be willing to pay once we arrive."

The man furrowed his brow. "See this road? It's the road out. See this car, it has everything I own. And we're stuck, have been for hours. You won't get a ride out because there's no riding."

"Could I plug in my phone for a minute?"

The man shook his head. "I can't spare the battery."

"Sure of course."

Beckett scanned up and down the jam of cars. Everyone seemed to be in the same shape. Even the motorcycles were stuck, slowly weaving through, and already carrying at least two people. Sometimes three.

And everyone glared as if they had been there for hours. Like they were pissed. Like he was invisible and they had lost all patience.

He found three guys in the back of a truck. "Spare some battery? Enough for me to make a call?"

"We need it for the trip."

"Okay. How long until the next town, from here."

"You mean in miles or days, because it looks like a week away from here."

"I suppose a ride is out of the question?"

"We paid. You got money?"

Beckett wanted to go west of course, but at this point, desperate, he would go East as long as a town was at the end of the road. He sighed and pointed in the opposite direction. "What about back there? Is there a town?"

One of the guys said, "Pretty far back," and pulled his hat down over his eyes signaling the conversation was over. Another truck passed by headed East.

Beckett climbed over the median wall to the other side of the road to hitch a ride the opposite way.

Trouble was the eastbound traffic was random. While Beckett had been talking to drivers in the westbound traffic, two or three trucks had passed headed east, but now that he needed one — nothing.

He guessed most supplies were traveling along the southern route, because this highway was still too close to the fighting, too unpredictable, for truckers to risk their loads. But these families, out here, with everything they owned were an emergency situation. As if to punctuate his thought, an explosion, somewhere north, jarred the earth. A scream went up from the traffic jam and horns blared. As if that would help. Two planes buzzed by overhead.

Beckett stepped back into the tree cover off the side of the road. And then surprisingly the horns did help. The cars inched forward and even gained a bit of speed. Now Beckett wished he had stayed on that side of the road, he could have jumped on a truck and held on.

He ate a bar — and then a truck came his direction. Beckett rushed to the road's shoulder and put out his thumb and when the truck failed to slow, waved his arms. The truck roared past him but then slowly stopped, right in the middle of the lane.

Beckett jogged toward it.

The driver put his head out the window. "You're headed the wrong way from safety."

Beckett said, "I need a ride to the closest town, I'm guessing it's this way."

"There's one up ahead." The truck driver didn't seem convinced he wanted to help.

Beckett said, "I've been on the front lines. Got my discharge papers a few days ago, I've hiked here, now I'm looking for transport home."

"Where's home?"

"Near Charlesville."

"Hoowee, you've got a long trip ahead of you especially if you go east to get there."

Beckett looked up and down the road. "I just need a town. Any town. A place to plug in my phone, to get a ride."

The driver paused for a second, his engine rumbling. "Fine. Get in. The next town this direction is forty-three miles."

Beckett grabbed his rucksack and jogged to the passenger side, opened the door and tossed his bag up and climbed in. "Thanks man."

"Sure, no problem. How long have you served?"

Beckett scrubbed his hand on his head. It felt good to be sitting down on a seat. He was damp still. He took off his raincoat and put it under his ass so he wouldn't get the guy's seat wet. "Six years, six months on the front."

"You're lucky to be begging for rides. You're also lucky someone with ethics and a strong patriotic belief system picked you up."

Beckett put his head back on the seat. "Yep. Lucky."

"You always been so lucky?"

Beckett opened one eye and looked at him. "If I was lucky, I don't think I would've spent a second on the front lines."

The man laughed. His laugh was low and had a hint of menace.

Beckett fished out his phone and checked it. Still no service. Almost dead. Beckett asked, "Did you serve on the front lines?"

The man smiled, gold tooth, missing tooth, fat cheeks, stubble. "Nope."

Beckett nodded and decided to continue to be conversational. "What are you transporting?"

The driver raised his brows with another chuckle. "This truck you just found your lucky ass in is full of munitions. So, you know, keep your ass in line." Laughing, he turned the radio on and cranked the volume up.

Chapter 7

Apparently Beckett fell asleep. The shitty music, the rumble of the truck, the lack of conversation, it all lulled him into relaxation, and he was passed out. He woke with a start a bit later and checked his phone again. It was at 1% and boom, dead. Okay, this super sucked.

"Got a way for me to charge my phone?"

The driver grunted and gestured at the port.

Beckett unwound his cord and plugged into the dashboard. "How much longer until town?"

"Bit longer, half hour, though there will probably be a blockade, so depends how long it takes to get through."

"I need to piss, can we pull over for a second?"

Without a word the driver pulled to the side of the road. The opposite side of the road was full of cars, jammed, honking, not moving again. It was about 7:30 pm, right at the edge of dark.

It was the time of day for looking at the horizon for the green flash of light, but trees, traffic, big truck, were all in the way. That green flash bullshit was too mystical for this moment, anyway. There was no way he was going to get the 'instructions to the world' right now, here, on the side of this road, headed in the wrong direction, with a surly ammunitions-carrying truck driver grunting beside him. Nope, this was surely a low point.

Beckett dropped from the truck to the gravel, walked toward the back tire, unzipped, and aimed his piss for the road by the back tire. He was about halfway through when the truck's tires spun out, the truck pulled onto the road, and drove away. Beckett struggled to zip his pants while chasing it. "Hey! Hey!!!! You've got my stuff! At least throw down my stuff!"

The driver waved a hand and kept going.

Beckett ran after the truck, full speed, but fast as he could go, the truck was faster, and the driver, though Beckett hoped at first, wasn't kidding. Beckett slowed, past able to catch the back bumper, out of breath — "Fuck!" He kicked gravel. "Fuck, fuck, fuck, fuck."

He put his hands on his head and looked up and down the east bound lane, then over the median at the completely immobile traffic jam on the westbound lane. "Fuck."

Okay maybe he was going to get the instructions to the world, and they would be: Screw you, Beckett.

He took stock. No phone. No water. His food was gone. Raincoat was on the seat. His entire sack with extra socks, toothbrush. All gone. He took a deep determined breath and began to walk.

Chapter 8

Chickadee and Roscoe returned late that night. She slammed through the front door and collapsed on the couch. "We didn't find him." She asked, "Dilly dearest, tea?"

It took Dilly about one minute to have tea mugs in front of all of them. Luna scooped the puppy up to her lap and scratched it hind the ears. "Where is he?"

Dilly dropped into a chair. She asked, "But that's good news, right? If he — if something — you would know, right?"

Roscoe said, "Yes, we would know. We've contacted the hospitals, his officers—"

"I've contacted my goddammed senator and if he doesn't give me answers by tomorrow, I'm going to the president," said Chickadee as she twisted trying to get comfortable in her chair.

Roscoe was watching her closely. "I'm sure you will Chickadee, but we've been told all the information they have. We have four people looking for him. We'll know something tomorrow."

Luna asked, "How far away is it?

Chickadee waved her away with a hand. "You don't want to go there dearest. It's the front lines, just war and mayhem, and too far away to get to."

Luna said quietly, "That's not what I mean, I think he's walking home."

Chickadee jumped up. "Walking home? Walking home from hundreds and hundreds of miles away? What makes you think that?"

"Because that's what I would do. I mean, I would paddle, but yes, I'd walk home."

Chickadee looked around at the faces, and turned to the front window, "How long? If he walked, how long?"

Luna shrugged. Roscoe shook his head. Dilly sighed.

"If he walked would he have enough food? And why wouldn't he call? And what if there are wild animals — is it through the woods?" Luna had never seen Chickadee like this, she sounded frantic, out of control.

Chickadee wandered into the kitchen, banging open doors and yank-crashing drawers. "What I don't understand is why haven't we heard anything? Could he be out — what if he's in a ravine?" A glass overturned with a glass-splintering crash. "Crap!" She called toward the living room, "Roscoe who should I call about this?"

Roscoe called back, "The spill? Or Beckett? Because I've called everyone. Now we have to wait."

It was as if Chickadee had turned a corner from her competent 'handling' of things and was now, incapable, and that was completely freaking Luna out.

Dilly stood. "Excuse me." She swooped into the kitchen speaking to Chickadee in a way that made Luna worry even more. "Now now, Chickie, take a deep breath, it will be okay."

Chickadee said, "No it won't, how can it be okay? I've done everything for that boy. I gave up so much to make sure he was safe and now—"

"He'll be okay, you need to try to tell yourself that. You're going to get yourself all worked up, and you won't be able to help if he needs help."

"What kind of help will he need, do you know what kind of help?"

"I don't, but I'm worried about you."

Chickadee said, "I just don't know what to do. If anything happened to that boy—"

"You're going to scare Luna, and me, and quite frankly yourself. You have to keep a clear head."

"I can't, I'm too terrified." Chickadee left the kitchen, stalked past Roscoe and Luna in the living room, and went to her bedroom slamming the door behind her.

Dilly returned to the living room. A look of worry passed between her and Roscoe.

Roscoe sighed. "I suspected a sinking was imminent."

"Me too," said Dilly.

Luna was stunned. She had never seen a look like that on Chickadee's face — despair. And something else, overwhelmed in an insurmountable way. She asked, "What's a sinking?"

"A sinking spell as Chickadee calls them. It looks like this one might be big." Roscoe clapped his hands on his thighs and rose with another sigh. "If you hear anything call. Also call me if there's anything I can do."

Dilly looked nervously at Chickadee's door. "And call me if you hear anything."

"Will do." Roscoe left through the screen door.

Luna asked, "Is Chickadee going to be okay?"

"She'll be fine, but she'll be in bed for a few days I suspect." Dilly stood and gathered tea mugs.

Luna asked, "I never saw her do that before."

"She wanted to hide it from you." She stopped and gave Luna a sad smile. "It will be up to me and you to run the place until her sinking spell is over. Shark needs a walk, too."

Luna said, "Oh — but there's a big storm coming . . ."

Dilly said vaguely, "Is that why it's so dark?" and disappeared into the kitchen, leaving Luna and Shark alone in the living room staring at Chickadee's shut door.

Chapter 9

Beckett climbed across the median to the lanes of cars sitting parked. He walked up to the first car, they had seen him chase the truck and seemed to think it was funny. "You got a phone I can —?"

The driver, laughing, rolled up the window.

Beckett looked up and down the stream of cars. And saw one with a young woman driving. The car was full, but all he needed now was a phone. He wove through the cars to her window and leaned. "Do you have a phone I can borrow, I was just robbed."

"Oh, just now?" She was pretty, long blonde hair. The girl beside her looked like a younger sister and the back seat was full with four older people crammed together.

"I lost everything. I need a phone to call home."

She glanced in the rearview mirror at the man in the backseat and handed her phone out the window.

Relief washed over Beckett.

—Finally, he would make contact with home, tell them what was happening. Chickadee would be able to figure this all out.

He pushed the phone icon and yes, there was service.

He stared down at the numbers. A blank stare.

The young woman was watching the confusion on his face — what was Chickadee's phone number? He had keyed it into his phone six years ago. Luna's phone was new. It had a three in it. He was pretty sure. What about Dilly's phone number? He punched in random numbers as panic started to rise. He deleted the random numbers and tried again picking numbers and now completely panicking — why the hell couldn't he remember any phone numbers?

The woman asked, "Are you having a problem?"

"No I just — I can't—" Beckett handed the phone back with his brain swirling for any idea what to do next. "I guess a ride west is out of the question?"

The man in the backseat said, "Definitely."

Chapter 10

Beckett spent the night on the side of the road, cold, hungry, tired. In the morning he walked east to the town. It was a tiny little shit hole full of squalor and dismay. A steady stream of cars weaved through it, escaping the coast, headed inland. To where? Simply in, going up, trying to get on.

Beckett's big plan was to wait at the gas station and beg, but the gas station was closed. Most every place was boarded up and shut down. In the entire town it seemed like four people were local and they each had the look in their eyes of Lost Everything and Well Beyond Hope.

People with that kind of look in their eyes would not be helpful. They would likely set themselves in the way of hope and help and any human kindness because when you lose everything there's a sense of justice in making someone else pay.

The town was full of street vendors selling food, trinkets, tools, and bottles of gas for a price. Beckett begged for food. For free. Please.

The answer was a resounding no.

And then when he found an older woman with a look that she had been kind once long ago, he asked, "Do you have any food to spare?"

And she answered, creatively, "What do I look like a restaurant?"

Which wasn't at all Beckett's question. Beckett wasn't looking for a restaurant. Restaurants cost money. He was looking for a nice person to take pity on him and give him some food and a place to sit down. Maybe let him borrow a phone so he could call his local law enforcement officials and tell them to sound the alarm with Chickadee and Roscoe.

He dumpster dived for food. In the past week there had been a lot of lows, but sitting hip deep in trash eating an old piece of bread had to be the lowest.

He slept on a bench. In the morning he found a driver who said, "Sure. I'll give you a ride, but no food. And if you seem suspicious in any way, creepy or talkative, you're out on the side of the road."

Beckett clenched his jaw. "That seems fair."

Chapter 11

Luna knocked on the bedroom door. "Chickadee?"

Chickadee grunted.

"Can I come in?"

"Yeah." Her voice was small and sounded far away. What happened to its boom? The room was dark. The big bed in the middle was covered in blankets that covered Chickadee's lump of a body in the middle. Her arm was thrown over her eyes.

Lightning lit up the room with a crackle, boom!

Luna yelped.

Chickadee asked, "What can I do for you?"

"I was wondering if I could stay in here for a bit until—"

"I usually just need to be alone."

"But Dilly is baking — and I was trying to be — and the storm—"

Chickadee peeled her arm off her face and peered down at Luna at the foot of the bed. "I don't think I can be any comfort, I'm really not capable right now."

"I know, but it's hard to be in a world where Chickadee isn't capable."

Chickadee sighed low and deep and dramatically, but Luna didn't leave. Couldn't leave. The storm had lit up the living room with a crash bang, and then Luna had gone to the kitchen, but Dilly had been busy and not helpful, distracted in a way Luna had never seen before, and now she was here — there was nowhere else. Chickadee asked, "Are you crying dear?"

Luna nodded. "I was thinking I could wait in here until—" Another lightning flash lit up the room.

Chickadee dropped her arm to the side and patted the bed. Luna scrambled up to the pillows, lifted the blankets and shoved her feet in, pulling them over her head. Chickadee said, "I can't promise I'll be the best company."

"That's okay, I'm just scared." Luna closed her eyes tight.

"Me too."

Luna asked from under the covers, "What are you scared of Chickadee?"

There was a long pause. Then Chickadee said, "What if I can't control what happens? What if I can't solve this?" Thunder boomed over the house rattling the windows. "What about you dear, what are you afraid of?"

Luna squeezed her eyes even tighter. "Everything."

Chickadee wrapped her arm around Luna's body. "Dear do you want to put your head on my arm?"

Luna shifted up and curled on Chickadee's shoulder. They both sat in silence for a while, listening to the deafening roar of the storm. Luna said, "I don't understand how to look for him. He boarded a boat and came looking for me. He found me. He saved me. And what am I doing? Nothing. Crying. Trying to convince Shark to stop chewing on my ankles."

"You're also growing a baby."

"In secret."

"Aargh. I hate feeling this impotent. Trouble is dear, I can't reason out what our next move is. Except going to the front lines, but Roscoe said I can't. I hate it when he's the voice of reason."

Luna's body shook with sobs. "I think I'll be all alone again."

Chickadee said, "Oh honey. You won't be. Ever."

Luna sniffled.

Chickadee said, "Dear, I never asked, and this might be the worst time, but how did you lose your family?"

Luna closed her eyes tight, clenched every muscle in her body, and had to force the words out. They broke free with a sob. "All at once." That was truly the whole story. And Luna's heart broke to speak the three words out loud. She cried long and hard, sobs wracking her body while Chickadee wrapped around her shoulders resting a cheek in Luna's hair.

Finally Luna relaxed, her breathing slowed, and after a while she fell asleep.

Hours later after the storm had passed, Luna woke up and looked around. It was about eleven at night. Chickadee was awake, a book open on her chest, a reading light pointing at a page.

Luna said, "I made your sleeve all soggy."

"Yes, and you took my perfectly good sinking spell, the one that was supposed to be all about me, and turned me all inside out so I spent it worrying over you. Now apparently I'm not sunk at all." Chickadee gave a Luna a sad smile.

"I'm sorry I ruined your terrible mood."

"All the girls are conspiring against me, smell that?"

Luna said, "Cookies."

"Damn right. Dilly is an evil genius."

Chapter 12

Beckett was finally headed west. He made it to the next town over, and now finally had a ride home. And though he knew almost everyone who lived on the mountain, it was a stranger who gave him a ride. Someone who never heard of Chickadee and didn't have her phone number. But it was just as well because he would be home in twenty minutes now. It was early afternoon.

So that was good.

The downside was that he was not good. He was exhausted.

The kind of bone-tired exhaustion that made him sore, causing his head to ache in a way that made him not able to think — just act and react — and pulled his face down into a grimace. The driver of the truck barely spoke to him, just pointed at the truck bed, leaving Beckett to guess he had become downright unpleasant to be around. When he passed a mirror, he looked five years older, and he was dirty in a way he couldn't fix easily. He needed a long shower, with soaps. No one had offered him a shower. He stunk.

His clothes were filthy.

His mouth hurt. Canker sores.

And he was pissed.

At the truck driver.

At the stupid army.

At the mother-fucking whole world — why did everything have to be so fucking stupid and mean all the goddamn time?

That was the litany going in his head.

Not — I'm almost home. I'm so happy. I can't wait to see Luna and tell her how much I love her — it was this:

I hate this. All of it, every goddam bit, and I am miserable.

That was all.

Chapter 13

Luna was expecting Roscoe to come for dinner hopefully bringing news, but in the meantime she planned to sit in the rocking chair and watch in the direction Beckett would come — to wait, hope, and will Beckett to walk up the drive.

She shoved through the screen door and forgot, brain too full of questions, to notice the door swing shut too slowly and the puppy to race out of the house. In one millisecond the puppy shot down the front steps.

Luna yelled, "Stop, puppy, Shark, Sharky, stop!" Shark spotted a small rabbit, skidded in a turn and bounded after it at full speed, into the underbrush of the woods with Luna screaming behind it, "Puppy! Shark! Puppy!"

Dilly and Chickadee heard the commotion and came racing out of the house, banging the screen and crashing down the steps. "Shark! Puppy! Sharky!"

But Shark wouldn't slow down. Shark continued on, barreling through the woods, headed up to the mountain top, with Luna in fast pursuit, Dilly just following, Chickadee lumbering up behind.

And that's why, after Beckett's ride deposited him at the end of the driveway, and he trudged up it to the house, there was no one home.

Chapter 14

Beckett stood on the front porch of his home. "Chickadee? Dilly? Luna!"

He needed food, water, to fall into a bed.

He was filthy though. He couldn't do anything until he washed, or wait — water first. Or wait — he needed — where was everyone?

This sucked, epically.

He made it home and no one was even here?

It seemed like the least they could do — be there. To greet him. Get him a glass of water. His boots were filthy. He had ridden in the bed of a truck like an animal, even though there were seats. Because he was so disgusting.

He needed someone to help him get his boots off so he could go inside to get some water.

Wait, there was a spigot in the back.

He tromped down the steps and through the weeds to the back of the house. He wanted to kneel down to get some water, but his thighs hurt, bad, like there was some serious vitamin deficiency going on, dehydration and whatever else. He dropped all the way down to the dirt, cranked on the water, rinsed his hands, and then cupped them and drank from them.

Across the field Chickadee, Luna, and Dilly, holding a squirming Shark, came strolling out of the woods, laughing, and almost looking carefree.

Beckett's attention was drawn to their laughter. He attempted to stand, knocked himself off balance, and stumbled, spilling water down his front and wetting his filthy pants.

He pulled himself to standing and — "Luna?"

Luna's smile fell. "Beckett, oh my god, Beckett!"

Chickadee boomed, "Beckie dearest!"

Dilly jogged with a jiggling Shark, calling, "Beckett!!!"

Beckett's brow furrowed, eyes focused on Luna's stomach. "Luna, what is —"

She skidded to a stop, said, "Ta-Dah!" and put up jazz hands.

This was not how she planned it. She had no idea why she did it — Ta-Dah? In hindsight, fast hindsight, while she was still shaking her jazzy hands, she already regretted it.

Beckett's face was stormy. He was a mess, a thunderclap of a human. "You're pregnant?"

He had an air of do-not-approach, so they pulled to a stop about ten feet away. Shark squirmed to get out of Dilly's arms.

Luna said, "Yes."

Sadly, the fact that they all froze, interrupting his homecoming with a distance of ten feet, made Beckett feel even more alone and unwanted, an uninvited houseguest. His heart beat fast and his color rose. He asked, "It's mine?"

Luna flinched. "Yes, of course."

Shark dropped to the ground and raced for Beckett's ankle, biting his boot, tugging at it.

Beckett stared at the dog as if he couldn't see it. His brain was rotating slowly, moving through this maze of information.

"How did you get home?" asked Chickadee. "We've been looking for you everywhere."

Beckett continued to stare at the dog. He mumbled, "I had to catch a ride. I got robbed, lost my phone." He shoved the puppy off his boots, but Shark growled and lunged forward again.

Beckett shook his head. "Luna, how long have you known?"

Luna's heart ached. Beckett was a heap of towering mess, and she wasn't holding him. She had missed her chance to hold him, and now that was it, she was stuck on the other side of a wall of Not Holding Him. "Since you left. I figured it out when I was sick the day you left."

He repeated, "When you were sick." He absentmindedly shoved the dog again.

Dilly broke her freeze and rushed forward. "Beckett we are so glad you're home, so glad. This is Shark, my new puppy. We need to get you inside. Get you fed." She dragged Shark by the collar toward the door.

Chickadee added, "Yes dear Beckie, you are thin as a rail. We need to feed you pronto." She grabbed Beckett by the arm and tried to tug him toward the front porch.

The trouble was though — Beckett couldn't breathe. He was stuck in a tempest of a full blown panic attack, but this time it was whipping his whole self, not just his breaths, he was whirling with fury. A hot storm rose from his chest.

He shook off Chickadee's hand. "You've known since you were sick the day I left? You've been pregnant this whole time, and you never told me Luna? You never said anything to me?"

40

Luna felt her own panic rise. This was not how it was supposed to go. There had been a chance he would be upset, but this was way worse than she had imagined. "I wanted to, I was going to tell you when you came home—"

"So it's my fault. I didn't come home, so I didn't get to know? You get to lie?"

Chickadee said, "It wasn't a lie Beckie. She wanted to tell you."

Beckett cocked his head. "When did you know Chickadee?"

"I knew the same day Luna knew."

"You let me get on a bus, go to fucking war, without telling me Luna was going to have a baby. You didn't think maybe I ought to know?" Beckett kicked at the mud sending a small splash onto his own boots.

"We were worried you would get in trouble. That you would come back."

Beckett nodded his head. He scowled. "Yeah, right, I get it. Beckett is just a dumbass. Beckett never does anything right. I mean look at me, only a dumbass can't get home from war. Can't make good decisions. Can't be trusted. A guy stole everything I had while I was taking a piss. So yeah, sure, you're right. I'm not to be trusted."

Dilly got the squirming Shark up to the porch, pulled it into the house, and jogged back to the yard to join the speechless others.

Luna said, "That's not—"

He turned on her. "I asked you over and over, are you okay, and you never mentioned you were pregnant, not once."

"I'm sorry, it seemed like the right thing—"

"Yeah, but here's the problem: you, my aunts, you've all been lying to me for months. Lying to me, everyone of you, so who here can't be trusted? That's what I want to know."

Luna said, "Oh Beckett it's not like that."

"It's exactly like that."

Chickadee stood taller. "Beckett the facts on the ground were such that we needed to help you get on the bus and go. We made a decision. It might not have been the best—"

"What if something had happened to Luna? To the baby? To me? Ever think of that?"

Dilly said, "Every day, we thought of it every day."

"But still. Lied." He looked down at the ground. He gulped his anger down, attempting to calm himself. Then he looked up, squinted. "Did any of you ever once think, hey, maybe if we tell Beckett, tell him Luna's going to have a baby, maybe he could apply for an early discharge, or I don't know, a not-on-the-front-lines-praying-and-reloading-and-holding -my-nut-sack-begging-the-universe-to-keep-me-alive deployment? Maybe Beckett could apply for a desk job — ever consider that?"

Chickadee dropped her hands to the side. "You could have done that?"

"Yeah, the Department of the Interior doesn't usually put new fathers on the front lines. It's the one nice thing they do, but you would have known if you would have been honest with me." He put his hands on his hips. "I can't believe this bullshit."

Luna said, "Beckett you're scaring me."

"Yeah, I'm sure I am. You know, fear is rampant. It's one of the things we all get to live with." He ran his hands over his face and up and around his head.

"Come inside, we'll talk this all out, explain." Chickadee put her hand on his arm again but Beckett brushed it off.

"No, I don't want to be here. Not anymore." He shoved past Luna and Dilly and trudged down the gravel drive. What were they doing crowding him in up against the side of the house, anyway?

Dilly said to his departing back, "Beckett, please."

He spun around red in the face. "I'm the most surprised by you, Dilly. We talked four or five times, really talked about what it was like for Luna, living here. You told me everything was okay, and I believed you. I didn't think you were capable of lying."

"I'm not. I—"

"Yeah, I need to not be here right now—" He stopped in mid sentence and stared down the driveway for a moment. Then he shook his head slowly. He turned back and spoke in a low even cold voice. "Does Dan fucking know?"

Tears streamed down Luna's face. "Yes."

"When did he find out?"

Luna opened and closed her mouth not wanting to say.

"Because he promised me. He promised, so he better not have known the whole time."

Chickadee said, "He wanted to tell you, but—"

"Fucking A, I knew it." Beckett spun around and stalked down the driveway away.

Luna said, "Oh god, oh no, what am I going to do?"

Dilly put an arm around her.

Chickadee raced toward the house. "Where are my keys?"

Chickadee. returned a minute later with a slam of the front door. She hustled by Luna and Dilly, started her car, and spun out of the driveway. She found Beckett trudging down the road, pulled beside him, rolled down the window, and begged, "Please get in the car Beckett. You need food. You need sleep, a bath. You'll feel better and—"

He continued walking, his jaw set.

"Think of Luna, think about your—"

Beckett stopped, bringing Chickadee's car to a halt. He said, staring straight ahead without looking at her, "I am so furious right now, I can't, just stop."

"But Beckett."

"Chickadee, stop."

She sat in the front seat of the car watching Beckett as walked down the road away.

Chapter 15

Beckett was even more furious when he arrived in the university town of San Dilamo. It had taken him two-and-a-half hours. He had forgotten to get money from home, or a phone, or anything. He had begged another ride. Nagging hunger pains were cramping his stomach. He stalked onto a university campus reeking and filthy. He was a nightmare come true. An embarrassment. Crappy part was how he was proving everyone right. He wasn't capable enough to handle this, clearly.

As he tromped down the highway, he thought of nothing but kicking Dan's smug, self righteous, buddy-bullshit down his throat. Because they had been friends. Beckett had believed so anyway.

He asked at the university and then requested help locating the marine science department. He read the directory, found Rebecca's office number, borrowed a phone, and called her. "It's me Beckett."

"Beckett!!!"

"Can I um have Dan's number?"

"Oh sure, how are you? We've been so worried. Dan and Sarah were frantic, I mean, we all were. How is Luna, cool news, huh? You're going to be a dad!"

He closed his eyes. *Going to be a dad.* "Yeah, cool news," he said. "When did you find out?"

She faltered at the coldness in his voice. "Oh — Dan and Sarah hid it from me for a few weeks, but I overheard them talking about it. We're all really excited." He didn't say anything, so she paused then carried on, "Dan and Sarah are both home right now."

Beckett leaned on a bulletin board covered in college fliers, scraps of paper, and coupons. "Can I get there on foot from the university?"

"Sure, it's a block over on College Row."

Beckett hung up without saying bye. He leaned his head against the wall, then forced himself to straighten up.

Chapter 16

Luna heard Chickadee's car door slam. She had been laying with her head cradled in Dilly's lap, having her hair stroked, comfortingly comforted, with soft sounds and soft pets. Except Shark was sharp and kept jumping up and snapping at her face.

She pushed the dog away and sat up and listened, but it was only one set of feet crossing the gravel drive, banging up the steps, crossing the porch, and yanking the screen door open.

Beckett wasn't with Chickadee.

Luna dropped her head back to Dilly's lap.

Chickadee bellowed, "What the hell is up with that boy?"

Dilly said, "Hush dear, don't scare . . ."

She didn't mention her, but Luna felt Dilly gesture toward her head. She needn't have bothered, Luna was already terrified.

She had lost Beckett.

He was gone.

She was alone.

Chickadee said, "Of course, of course . . ."

Luna blew out a deep gust of breath and sat up. "It's okay, talk freely."

"I don't want to scare you dear, but oh, what is that boy thinking?" Chickadee dropped into a chair and then stood up again. "He has never in all my life, in all his life — I gave up so much to come here and take care of that boy and this is the thanks I get?"

She stalked into the kitchen and banged things around. Returning a few minutes later with a bag of potato chips with, "Crunchy Good," printed on the bag. She gripped the sides and ripped it open with a popping burst of cheese powder and stuffed a handful in her mouth. "He comes home and then races away, angry—what the hell is he thinking? None of this makes sense."

Luna asked, "Is he coming back?"

"Well, I don't know, I can't tell what's in his mind. I've a half a mind to tell him not to bother." Chickadee collapsed in her favorite chair with a huff and absentmindedly put her fingers down so Shark could lick the cheese off her fingers.

Dilly said, "You don't mean that."

"I do. I've never heard of anyone being so ungrateful, so insolent, such a boneheaded twerp of epic proportions."

A tear rolled down Luna's face.

"This is what I mean," said Dilly, "you're scaring Luna."

Chickadee glanced at Luna and her face softened. "Dear, this is nothing to worry about — but I can't believe my nephew would give you one second of pain. He is going to rue this day."

Luna asked, "If he doesn't come home, what am I going to do?"

Dilly and Chickadee conferred in a glance. Dilly said, "You'll live here. You'll be a part of our family the way you already are. This is just a silly—"

Chickadee said, "Yes of course, Luna, you'll always live here, this is your home, but Dilly this is not silly. I don't understand what this is, but silly is not a good descriptor."

"You're right," said Dilly. "Silly is not the right word, but perhaps hiccup, or better yet, screw up, this is merely a screw up. That's a good word for what this is."

Luna was mentally packing, planning. She would take her clothes, pack the gear that was in the south barn, her paddleboard. She would find a ride to Heighton Port and put out to sea. She would head northwest in search of Sky. She could probably accomplish that in a month. Then she'd still have time to plan where she would go to nest for the baby. Her hand rested on her rounded stomach while she listed practical things, like how much food she would need for the trip and how to get a ride to the port.

While Luna was mentally listing, Chickadee said to Dilly, "You're making it sound inconsequential, like our nephew, Beckie, didn't storm around here like a total ass. Maybe you understand what this is about, but if you have some special insight, perhaps you should share it with me. And preferably before I have a stroke." She shoved another handful of chips in her mouth, her eyes half-crazed, faded-to-moss-green mohawk sticking up in all directions.

Dilly said, "It's simply his expectations didn't match up with his longing, so he freaked. That's all that was. A freak out."

"That was more than a freak out, and what do you mean expectations? I told you, stroke happening, my goddamned blood is going to shut down my synapses and then where will you be, dear Dilly. Where. Will. You. Be?"

"Hopefully with someone who actually stops talking long enough to hear what other people are saying."

Chickadee glared at Dilly. It was the closest to a fight Luna had ever seen them get. She stopped mentally listing her plans for an escape route and listened, mouth agape.

Chickadee took a second to brush her cheddar fingers on her pants. "Fine, dearest one, I'll be quiet while you enlighten me."

Dilly said, "Well—"

"But if I have a stroke in silence, it's your fault." Chickadee stuck out her tongue.

Dilly raised her brow and shook her head. "Beckett has gone through something so awful, so soul crushingly awful, and — how many days ago did he disappear?"

Luna said, "Too many."

"Exactly. And his dream of home, the dream that got him here, after all that ordeal, well that dream didn't materialize when he was standing in the yard drinking out of the spigot. He thought he was coming home to one thing, but we greeted him with another. And the thing was, from the looks of him, there was all primal animal stuff going on in his brain, the kind of pain and anger of a wounded dog, and we could have greeted him with a tray of his favorite cookies, but we probably still wouldn't have done it right."

Chickadee huffed. "You're saying we didn't bake the right cookies?"

"I'm saying Beckett tried to come home and he couldn't actually do it. He was too frightened of all the things that had changed. He needs a do-over. After he cools down, has something to eat—"

Luna said, "At Dan's."

"Precisely. And then Beckett will try again."

Chickadee asked, "Love, how do you know all that?"

"Because he told me, in his eyes, when he said, 'Dilly, I'm the most disappointed in you.' I got what he was saying. You've only got to listen."

Luna said, "But how do you know he'll try again?"

Dilly hugged her arm around Luna. "Because you're here, sweetie. He'll come home for you."

Luna nodded. "So I'm going to wait on the porch."

Dilly said, "And I'm going to bake some more cookies, they solve everything."

Chapter 17

He banged on their front door. "Dan, it's me Beckett!"

Dan opened the door with a, "Welcome home Army!" then, "Phew! You look like hell man."

"I want my keys to my bike."

"Whoa, what's with the — you been home? You heard?"

"Yeah, I heard."

"So what's with the attitude?"

"The attitude? My attitude?" Beckett's volume climbed. "I just got home from a six months front-line deployment to find my girlfriend, my family, and you, everyone, lying to me."

Dan looked left and right down the hall. "How about you come in?"

"Screw that. I want my keys."

"Come in the house Army. I'll get you the keys."

Beckett stepped through the door to the hallway. Sarah appeared around the corner. "Beckett! You're home!"

He scowled.

She glanced at Dan who said, "Beckett's going to wait here while I go get him his keys, cool?"

"Yeah, um, okay." Sarah backed out of the hall. Beckett stood silently, his breath rasping in his throat, his hands clenched into fists, watching her back away.

Dan disappeared after her calling over his shoulder. "So you've been home? You don't look like someone who's been home. And you stink like a fish in the sun."

"My keys." Beckett's voice was clipped, commanding, erupting from within his madness, the aroma of a cooked meal was wafting down the hall, drifting into his lungs, making his stomach want to scream.

From a distant room Dan called, "Sure. Sure."

Beckett shifted from foot to foot listening to Dan rummaging. Then Dan emerged carrying the keys, "See, just had to get them," dangling them in front of Beckett's face.

Beckett glowered and reached, but Dan yanked them away. "Nope — not giving it back. Not until you talk to me."

Beckett shook his head slowly from side to side. "You're making a mistake man. We were friends. I can't believe you're such an ass."

"We are friends. Let me prove it to you." Dan gestured toward the end of the hall. "Come to the kitchen. I bet you miss my cooking."

Beckett considered wrestling the keys away. He'd shove Dan against the wall and take them, his fists ached with the want of it. Beating someone, anyone, Dan, would be a relief. He was too mired in pain to pull up out of it — like a drowning man flailing in stormy waves, he wanted to lash out, cause more, make it worse.

Dan said, "Here's the thing, I made some food. It's good too, pasta, marinara, meatballs. You'll like it, warm and—"

Beckett's stomach-brain overtook his animal-brain. He all but growled when he spoke. "I'll come in for one minute, for food, but I want my keys." He stalked by Dan down the hall. When he stepped into the kitchen Sarah was already filling a plate with pasta and red sauce. She gestured to a chair and without a word placed the plate in front of it. She filled a glass with ice and water and set it beside the plate and tossed down some utensils.

Dan slid into a chair across from Beckett and began to eat.

Sarah sat down beside them and began to eat.

Beckett was so thirsty he had to tend to that first. He grabbed the glass, drained it, set it down, and stared at a spot in the middle of the table while Dan refilled it. Beckett gulped it down. He needed more water, but he was too famished now, hands shaking, past hungry to near fainting. He had worked through the hunger with pure furious angst until he'd almost forgotten, but now he remembered. It hit him with a full force punch in the stomach. He had to have food. He couldn't be ceremonious, or dignified, or even refuse out of anger. He ripped the bread in half, stuffed it in his mouth, chewed twice and swallowed, then devoured the pasta with big gulps of heaping forkfuls. Dan and Sarah exchanged a glance and ate quietly.

When Beckett got to the end of the plate, Dan jumped up, spooned another giant helping onto it, and pushed it back in front of Beckett who looked at it dazed. Then he picked up his fork and ate that plateful too.

Finished, Beckett got up with a slam, carried his plate to the sink, washed it angrily, and returned to stand behind his chair. "Thank you for the food, as you can see, it had been awhile, but it doesn't change anything. I want my keys so I can go."

Dan, elbows on the table, still holding his fork asked, "Where you going?"

"I don't know. Somewhere else."

Dan nodded, scrutinizing Beckett's face. "What did Luna say when you told her you were leaving?"

Beckett stood for a second glaring at Dan then he shook his head. "I don't know, nothing, she didn't—"

"She said nothing? You told her you were leaving, and she just said nothing?"

Beckett looked down and shook his head. "It didn't get that far, I left—"

"You left angry. You came home from war, saw Luna, and left angry, and now you're here, running away. Where you going, man? Your home is back there."

Beckett's jaw clenched and unclenched.

"Beckett, I need you to sit down, so we can talk this out before you go."

"I can't. I just —" Beckett gripped the back of the chair, twisting on the wood. "I don't know what I'm doing. I just—"

Dan shoved the chair back from the table with his foot and gestured for Beckett to sit down.

The force of the chair shoving into Beckett's front caused a collapse, of his straight up fury, spine, legs. Beckett dropped into the seat. "I don't know what I'm doing at all."

Dan said, "True that."

"What am I going to do?" Beckett put his elbows on the table and dropped his head in his hands. Sarah got up quietly and left the room.

Dan dragged his own chair around the table, closer, put his hand on Beckett shoulder, and bowed his head. "I'm not sure which part of your tragic life you're questioning — the friends rallying around you, the aunts who adore you, Luna? The baby that is coming? Your baby, man. A baby. And I haven't known you for long, but you seem to be the kind of guy who pulls your shit together when called on. You found Luna in the ocean. You lived on an Outpost. But look at you now."

Beckett clamped his eyes shut. "I screwed up royally. I wasn't thinking . . . I was just so mad." His head hung low between his shoulders.

"Anger isn't bringing out the best in you." Their voices were quiet, ear to ear, voices filling the tight space between them.

"I haven't been the best me for a long, long time." A tear rolled down Beckett's nose, into his lap, between the two men's knees.

Dan wrapped a hand around the back of Beckett's head. The side of his forehead pressed to Beckett's forehead. "It's time to change that, you've got a baby on the way."

"How can I bring a baby into this hellhole of a world? We aren't winning this war. The water is coming."

Dan nodded, warm stubble scratching against Beckett's cheek.

"Did you hear the eastern ridges are burning?"

Dan said, "No man, I didn't."

"They are, they're fucking burning, the whole forest. The roads are full of refugees, crawling in cars, hiking on foot, walking away from the fires, headed from the interior to one coast and then the other coast where guess what awaits them?"

Dan said, "Water."

"Water, hot stagnant, the land over crowded, and people will get sick, and die, and I can't figure out how to keep on . . ."

Dan said, "Me neither. I can't imagine finding any hope in that scenario."

Beckett leaned back in his seat, Dan remained leaned forward, forearms on his knees. Beckett said, "I got on that bus. I met my regiment, and then we were deployed to protect the power plants. Six years without any combat and suddenly, I'm fighting. They dropped our asses in the zone and told us to defend it with our lives."

"That sucks."

"The only thing that saved my ass was that no one was dropping the big bombs, got to protect the resources. It was street by street, hand to hand sometimes. Trying to get to the top of buildings so I could shoot from above . . . God."

Dan stared down at his hands. "That sounds awful."

"It seemed like every day I had to do something worse than the day before."

"You never mentioned you were away fighting in the east, we didn't know."

Beckett sighed. "I didn't tell you, didn't want to worry you."

"Same."

"I feel like it's different though. That shit I was doing was better left unmentioned. Luna on the other hand, a baby, someone should have told me."

Dan nudged the water glass within Beckett's reach. "I screwed up. Luna screwed up. Your aunts. All I can say, in our defense, we were trying to help you."

Beckett balked, and Dan put up his hands. "I get it, it's uncool to say it like that. We knew you were miserable, and we wanted to take some of the load off of you. Knowing Luna was pregnant, and you couldn't be there, seemed like too big a load."

Beckett nodded. He gulped down the full glass of water, placed it on the table, and spun it a couple of times, thinking. "I see that. It was still wrong, but I have been in a load of trouble for months. And then getting home. Getting home was . . ." Beckett shook his head slowly, remembering it in vivid detail. "I got robbed, get this — while my pants were down around my ankles, taking a piss."

"Wow Army, I don't even know where to begin with that. I imagine that's got to be the bottom."

"Maybe. But maybe the depths will keep getting deeper. The water is coming. We're all just scrambling for higher ground." Beckett looked in Dan's face for the first time since he had arrived. "And that's what I mean, what am I going to do? How am I going to scramble with a family?"

"You've always had a family. It's just getting bigger."

Beckett moaned.

"You need to talk to Luna."

"God, Luna, how is she ever going to forgive me?"

"Probably the way every man who deserves it gets forgiven, by begging for it."

"Imagine how she feels after what I just pulled."

Dan nodded. "I can imagine, but she loves you. And she needs you. I think you'll be able to work it out."

"Phew." Beckett shook his head slowly.

"Yep. Phew is right."

"A baby?"

"A baby. And if I haven't made it clear, I'm really sorry I didn't tell you. I didn't think you could handle the news, but look at you, practically a professional."

A sad smile spread across Beckett's face. "I've proven I'm good at handling things?"

Dan clapped his hand down on the table with a chuckle. "That was total sarcasm my friend, you apparently can't handle much at all. You stink like garbage, you're dirty, practically muddy — is that a flea on your head? How can you be at my table like this? Thankfully the girl carrying your baby can handle anything life throws at her."

"Yes I suppose that's true." Beckett's smile faded. "So, can I have my keys now?"

Dan said, "After you shower. With vigor."

Chapter 18

After Beckett raced away on his motorcycle, Dan called Luna. "He's on his way back to you, and I don't want to say much. Don't want him to think we're in collusion again, but I believe you should give him a—"

Luna said, "Yeah, I get it, I agree. I'm waiting for him on the porch. And yes, I agree. Thank you for calling."

"He's showered too, you're welcome."

Luna hung up and stared out over the driveway. She had made a promise to herself she wouldn't look away.

Chapter 19

Beckett's arms shook from the effort of the drive. He was exhausted. More than exhausted physically although the physical exhaustion had been enough. Traffic had been terrible, stop and go, and during the stops he had trouble keeping his head from lolling forward. How would that have been to fall asleep astride his motorcycle in the middle of the road? After that he had tried not to stop, to ride up the shoulder, and weave in and out of the parked cars.

One hundred percent he should have spent the night at Dan's. There was no reason at all for him to be on the road in his condition. But also every reason. He couldn't sleep, not until he fixed this mess he had made. Unbreak all the hearts.

But worse than physical, he was emotionally exhausted. He knew he needed to talk this out, explain himself, beg for forgiveness and make amends, but he couldn't imagine having the strength for any of that. But he had to. Even though he wanted to curl up in a ball and do nothing but sleep for the next week. He had to make this all better.

Leave it to someone in a big damn mess to make it twice as big. He was a dumbass. He had been trying not to be, but there was no denying it.

About half way home the rain started. The road began to wind up the mountain. The visibility went to almost zero. His only good luck in days was that Dan had loaned him a raincoat. Unluckily, he couldn't keep it over his knees. Sopping didn't go far enough to describe how wet he was.

Chapter 20

Luna waited. The porch was wide and wonderful, her favorite place. Dark and cool on hot days, sheltering on rainy days. It had a couch covered with pillows for lounging. She had imagined many a day that she would lie there wrapped around Beckett. It was a goal. There was also two beautiful rocking chairs. Sitting in them reminded Luna of being on the water. She lolled on them. Like spinning in a current with twists, she rocked, eyes out on the horizon, over the valley toward the direction of the sea. She had to use her imagination to see it, but she could imagine it glinting. Waiting.

Also coming closer. She could just wait here and the water would come. But she reminded herself not to say that to Beckett. Ever. And really, the side of this mountain, they were safe. If one wanted to be as far away from the water as one could be, this house was the place.

Now she wasn't lolling, she was actively waiting, with her whole body, stiff, alert, listening. She pet Shark while he slept, and when he started biting her hands, wrists, elbows, and feet, tossed him into his crate 'to rest' because sometimes, "Sharky needed a break," as Dilly would say. Which meant they were all exhausted by the little puppy's demanding personality. Luna did not want Beckett to be greeted by Shark this time. He would get to meet the puppy on his own terms.

It began to rain. A warm downpour, drenching and loud. Beckett was on a motorcycle in this mess. So she added worrying to actively waiting.

Chapter 21

Beckett's wheels churned up the driveway's gravel. He pulled close to the porch, but could still barely see the house — except lights were on. That was good, they would be home. This time. He shook his head, helmet rocking on his shoulder, rain pouring down the visor. He swung his leg off the bike, pulled the helmet off, and turned to the porch — there — Luna.

She stood at the top of the steps, under the roof, just outside of the rain, beautiful. He dropped to his knees. Right there in the mud. Rain rolling down his face in rivers, raincoat hem in the puddles, helmet falling to the ground with a splash. He was collapsed with the pain of his inside torture. "I'm so sorry." He had to say it loud because the rain was deafening, all-surrounding, isolating.

Luna stepped down to the bottom step and grabbed ahold of him, wrapping around his head, clutching him to her rounded stomach. Rivulets of warm water gushed down their bodies. She held him tight.

He wrapped his arms around her back, holding, pulling her closer, crying into her stomach — he begged again, "I'm sorry, God, I'm so sorry."

His hold was intense, strong, pulling, holding her so close and tightly as if he wanted to pull inside her body or pull her inside his — "I didn't mean it. I'm sorry." Their separation had been too long. He felt foreign to her, rejected. He wanted, needed, to crawl inside her, make her his home.

The strength of his need forced her back — she collapsed down to the bottom step with a splash. Leaned on his arms, she wrapped her legs around his waist, and clutched the back of his raincoat, pulling him even closer. His boots shoved into the mud, pushing him forward, climbing her body. The rain poured down, obscuring sound, sight, thought. There was only Luna under Beckett, the two wrapped tight around each other in the rain.

"I didn't mean it." His words were drowned by the water. His boots shoved into the mud. Propelling him forward. Holding. Tightening. "I love you." He nuzzled into her shirt, her chest. His face hidden from sight, his words spoken into her skin. "Please forgive me. I'm so sorry."

Then his shoulders shook with the pain and rage of the last days.

She held on, within his arms, feeling the force of his quaking, cracking, heart, soul, body, and waited, for his terrible energy to dissipate.

He stopped pulling and pushing, climbing and begging, and stilled, finally, sopping wet, drenched through, boots dug into the mud, but finally still.

And then with deep low breaths they stayed there, Luna holding Beckett on the steps to his home, the never ending water pouring down.

Luna's hands rubbed down and around the rubberized raincoat on his back. She stroked the stubble on the back of his head and lifted her head to kiss the top of his.

After a few more moments he said, "I'm sorry."

Luna stroked her fingertips down his jawline and pulled up his chin. There was pain and sadness and fear in his eyes, but in his cheek, under her fingertips, held the promise of his dimples. She could barely remember the last time those dimples had been aimed at her — but that was a lie. How could she forget their last morning together? He was looking down over the railing of the ship as she paddled. His eyes full of awe and love and a smile that said it all, full dimples shining — he was happiest with her. That much was true.

In answer to his I'm sorry she said, "Welcome home."

He nestled into her chest again and his shoulders heaved again with tears, so she held him even longer.

Until it was, as Chickadee later said when they were able to smile about it all, "Absolutely ridiculous how long you two spent out there in the rain."

Beckett was spent by the emotions, the ordeal, the mess, and the trauma. His body gave up in a way, and he went soft and heavy and almost fell asleep right there with Luna's legs wrapped around him, his boots shoved into the mud, and rain pouring down his back. But just at that moment when he was perfectly halfway between wake and sleep, like that moment of sunset when the clarity of the green flash answers all the questions, wham — the baby, a new being that hadn't even been addressed or barely noticed, kicked.

Beckett jerked up, shocked and confused for a moment. "Whoa, Luna." His hand reflexively went to her stomach, but hovered an inch above. He looked up at her face, his eyes wide.

She nodded.

He slowly placed his hand on her stomach.

She said, "Wait there."

And after a moment the baby rolled from one side of her stomach, jutting, rolling back across to the other side, a lump jutted out, and then disappeared.

"Does that always happen?"

"Only when the baby is awake. It probably heard your voice."

Beckett looked down at her stomach, accepting that as true. "We need to get you out of the rain."

Chapter 22

As soon as Beckett and Luna's feet hit the top step of the porch, Dilly and Chickadee bustled out of the house and wordlessly wrapped Beckett and Luna up in towels. You could tell they were trying to be exuberant, yet cool and not talk too much. Beckett asked, "Forgive me, Chickadee? Dilly? I'm so sorry."

Chickadee said, "For what dear boy?" Then she chuckled. "Okay, fine, I can't pretend that wasn't an awful homecoming, you were a total ass, but of course, forgiven. What about you Dilly?"

Dilly smiled. "For what dear boy?"

Beckett swept them up in his arms and gave them a sopping wet hug. When Chickadee was released, she brusquely rubbed at his hair with another towel. "You are such a sight for sore eyes, look at you!" She threw her arms around him, and he buried his face in her shoulder. "I can't believe you're home."

Beckett was led into the laundry room off the kitchen to sponge and towel off and put on warm clean clothes. He emerged a while later in sweat pants and a t-shirt and bare feet. He had missed bare feet. He had begged off on a shower saying he had taken one at Dan's and, "This is entirely too much wet. No more wet."

Luna did disappear to hop in a warm shower and change into dry clothes, so when she returned Beckett was at the kitchen table, leaned on an elbow tiredly chewing a cookie and alternately yawning while Chickadee beamed at him, holding one of his arms saying, "—a new tattoo?"

Beckett looked down, yawned loudly. "I added a butterfly."

"It's beautiful."

Luna stopped in the door, the scene was so warm and domestic and happy and perfect — except for Beckett's yawns — she wanted to memorize it. Beckett was home.

Dilly busied herself with a cup of tea. "Beckie, I've been collecting Thai recipes and have the whole week's menus planned."

"Good, because I'm the kind of hungry that will take about twenty-one meals to fix."

Dilly appraised him. "You are very very thin, but we'll fix you right up."

Luna pulled a chair up beside him and leaned back watching him. Beckett extended a hand, entwined his fingers through hers in her lap, and looked back at her with his dimpled smile. Her heart soared. Beckett was home and she was home.

"Also, not too spicy, my mouth has sores inside."

Chickadee dropped her spoon. "Are you okay? Do you need a doctor?"

Dilly said, "He's fine, right Beckett? A vitamin deficiency, we'll get him fixed right up."

"Well, I'm calling my senator. He's in worse shape then when he left. It's unconscionable."

"Chickadee, you had any sinkings while I was gone?"

"Just one." Chickadee glanced at Dilly. "Okay two, but the second one was short, Luna helped me."

"That's nice." Beckett squeezed Luna's hand and yawned.

Dilly asked, "Do you need anything else Beckett? I made—"

But Beckett, without taking his eyes from Luna said, "Nah, I'm good." He pulled Luna's arm up under his, and she entwined around his bicep leaning her head on his shoulder.

Dilly busied herself putting away food, and Chickadee jumped up to make a pot of coffee, and Beckett whispered, his breath hot on Luna's cheek, "I'm so tired, but I had a whole plan that included making love to you, and now you're pregnant and—"

She said, "We still can."

"We can? Even though?"

Luna nodded.

"Okay then." Beckett pushed his chair back. "Dilly and Chickadee, thank you, I love you, good night." He stood, groaned, and pretended to struggle to heave Luna up from her chair.

Luna giggled. "You're such a weakling." She stood up on her chair and climbed on Beckett, wrapping her legs around his waist. He wrapped his hands around her thighs, buried his mouth in her neck, and carried her out of the kitchen.

Luna looked out over his shoulder at Chickadee, laughing, while Dilly shook her head with a smile.

Chapter 23

Beckett carried Luna through the living room toward the door of his bedroom, but Luna flung out a hand, grabbed the door jamb, and pulled them to a stop. He asked, "What?"

"Let's go in my room."

"Your room? What, the guest room?"

Luna nodded.

Beckett opened that door by pushing Luna's butt against it. The guest room had been a place to store stuff, plus the crafting room, and also the storing of random furniture and knickknacks, but now it had been painted white with a large bed at the end covered in white bedding and pillows. White curtains hung in the window and a small table stood against the wall, spare and clean.

He looked around his lips still pressed on her neck. "It looks great."

She dropped her toes to the floor and pulled his shirt over his shoulders and off over his head. She kissed his chest. "I missed you." She ran her hands down his shoulders. He was thinner, his muscles sinewy, taut under the skin.

He shoved her door closed with his foot and in the same moment pulled her shirt off, cupping his hands around her breasts, and moaning. He kissed down her neck to her shoulder and rubbed his hands down her back and into the top of her yoga pants and shoved them down and off her legs. "God, you're naked."

Luna smiled.

He picked her up. She wrapped her legs around his waist again, and he dropped her onto the bed. She shoved the top covers down while he took off his pants. He looked down at her, spread eagled across the fluffy white comforter, her body familiar and longed for, different, but so beautiful. He felt dizzy at the thought of her. He clamped his eyes closed and dropped beside her legs and hugged her hips. "I missed you."

"I missed you too." She looked down at him. His eyes were closed. She wondered if he might fall asleep, there wrapped around her bottom half. But instead he kissed her hip and then her thigh. "I missed these legs. This kneecap."

"My kneecap missed you too."

He shifted and wiggled down to her feet. "I missed this ankle bone."

Luna joked, "You did? Because I didn't think you'd been properly introduced."

He licked it with a laugh. "There, me and Luna's anklebone are best friends." He climbed up her body, stroking along her legs and talking about how much he missed her small parts, but mentioning especially how much he had missed the soft place between her legs, and playing there, until Luna moaned, "Oh, Beckett," as waves rolled through her body.

He slowly climbed his way up, stroking and kissing, and jokingly introducing himself to all her soft curves, until he was face to face and then he stilled. His eyes were deep and searching. "I'm so sorry." He kissed her lips.

She wanted him so much her breath had gone with a gasp. "I know you are, and I've forgiven you." She ran her hands down his back, pulling him closer, pressing against him. "But Beckett if you keep saying it, I'll roll out from under you, and you'll have to start over introducing yourself to ankle again."

Beckett chuckled. "I'd never be able to start over. I can barely remember my own name."

"You're Beckett, meet Luna." And then they made love, in a bed for the first time, on land, at home — until Beckett's breath caught — he groaned into her ear and pulled her closer burying his face into the skin between her shoulder and her throat. He moaned again, kissing there. Luna pressed against him more until finally he fully relaxed away.

Luna stretched her arms over her head. "That was awesome."

He dropped his head to the pillow. "In my imagination I made love to you for eight hours straight. I think I just lasted about six minutes." He gave her a sad smile.

She grinned. "But those six minutes were epic. Also I lasted for two."

She ran her fingers down his cheek, looking at his eyes, his skin, his nose, his lips, memorizing every spot and line. She said, "How can I love you so much but also feel like I'm seeing you for the first time?"

He smiled. "Because both of those things are true."

She ran her hands through the shaggy hair on his head and down his neck, up his shoulder and down his arm. She paused there for a few minutes, tracing the redwood trees tattooed on his arms and whispered, full of awe, "This butterfly is for me?"

He nodded watching her eyes. "It's the Monarch, above the trees, carrying our whispers."

She held his palm open and traced a finger along the scar. She massaged the callouses and brought the fingers to her lips and kissed them. She placed his hand on her chest just over her heart, and then led his hand down her chest to the bottom of her stomach and pressed it there, just as the baby squirmed.

Beckett's eyes went wide. "That is so amazing."

She nodded. "It's a miracle." The baby kicked again.

"I'm stunned." Beckett slowly shook his head.

"You're handing it very well, considering."

"I want to joke and say something like, 'I don't know if you noticed but while I was away, something took up residence in your pelvis.' But joking at a time like this seems barbaric. So instead of joking I have questions. A lot of questions. Idiotic questions. And so I'm going to ask again, and I may keep asking — you're pregnant?"

"I'm pregnant."

"I don't think I've ever known anyone who was pregnant before."

"I've known two people in my life."

"I don't want to sound like a total monster, but I needed sex so badly I couldn't think, or talk, and now that's over I need sleep. I'm having trouble concentrating. You're pregnant?"

"Yes. Almost seven months."

"Pregnancies last for nine months?"

"Really ten. Because the people who first started counting couldn't count very well."

Beckett sat quietly for a moment counting in his head: days, hours, weeks, months. He had no idea what he would have to accomplish in that time, but he imagined it would take all the strength and courage he could muster, but again his brain was a jumble. So he said, dumbly, "You're really pregnant?"

"Yes," she answered, knowing she was answering a lot more.

"I don't know if I mentioned before, but also in my imagination, I'm not leaving bed for about three days." He pulled the covers to his waist, covering Luna's rounded stomach. He replaced his hand on the lower part of her belly again, watching and waiting for the movement.

"We can stay here as long as you want, I think Dilly and Chickadee are planning to feed us in bed for a month, anyway."

"How are you getting along with them?"

"Really great. They are . . ." She paused. "I don't know how to say it, because great isn't good enough. They're perfect. If I had to pick a new family, they would be the ones, you know?"

"I'm glad. They are great, and I'm happy to share them." The baby kicked Beckett's hand again and his eyes widened. He watched her tummy and finally he laid back on the pillow. "Why did you get your own room?"

Luna turned to her side and looked down at him. "I slept in your room in the beginning. But it's so full of your things, your memories and trophies and books and photos."

He groaned. "I didn't know you were coming, I — I'm sorry about that."

"It's not a big deal, it just felt weird. I was a guest in someone else's room — a stranger's room. The first few nights it didn't bother me because I was so tired and so relieved to be inside, but then it bothered me. One morning Dilly asked if I was okay, and I couldn't explain what was wrong. We talked it over and figured out that without you there to explain what things were or meant I was turning you into a stranger.

That day Dilly cleaned out the guest room and she and I decorated it and turned it into mine. You weren't a stranger anymore. I could go back to thinking about you, my Beckett, that I love, and you were coming home to me, and I was a part of your family. I know you. The present you. Not the past you."

Beckett said simply, "Remind me Dilly deserves an extra hug when I see her next time. Possibly in five days." He pulled Luna to his chest. "And I like this room better. The window faces west."

She traced a circle around and around on his chest. "Maybe while you're here, you can introduce me to some of your things. So I know a little bit about the past Beckett too." Her voice caught in her throat.

He raised her chin to look up at him. "We're doing this different you and I. We fell in love before we got to know each other. I loved you before I knew your name. You loved me before you knew you would live long enough to tell me. But that doesn't make it wrong or destined to fail. That just means this is different."

"More magical?"

"Yes, magical." He kissed the top of her hair and mumbled something about 'love you' and then he went quiet. His body stilled and slowly Beckett fell asleep.

Luna remained awake.

The rain continued to pour.

Chapter 24

Six hours later Beckett woke and looked around. It was minutes before dawn and he needed to sleep more. He glanced to his right and Luna was watching him. "Hi."

He said, "You aren't sleeping?"

"Nope." She curled up. "I have to keep checking you're really here."

"Good, because I need a lot more sleep and I'll do it better if someone is watching." He grinned. Then he wriggled down, so he was face level to Luna's belly, nose to belly button. "Remind me again, there's a baby in there?"

Luna smiled. "Yep. Baby dances while I'm sleeping."

Beckett rested his hand on the side. "It's so beautiful—" A lump protruded from the side of her rounded stomach knocking his hand. "And weird." He ran his hand down along her hip.

"I have stretch marks now."

He kissed her stomach. "You've always had those, and they're beautiful, and I don't remember how you looked before." Then he said, "Nah, I'm lying. I'll never forget how you looked that night on the Outpost when you stripped all your clothes off standing over me. That was — but this is amazing too."

Luna stroked her fingers through his hair. "I made a big impression that night, huh?"

"Yep." He continued to stroke his hands up her thigh and her hip to her belly and back down.

"And we made a baby."

"We did. And I knew it, that night on the Outpost, I knew something big had happened. I didn't understand it, but here we are."

"Curled up in bed together in your mountain house."

"Our mountain house."

Luna looked down at him. "Oh."

"I was thinking—" He wriggled back up to put his head on the pillow and eye to eye. "That we should get married. Or wait — Luna, will you marry me?"

Luna smiled. "Marry you? You haven't even had a full night's sleep."

"I don't need a full night's sleep to know I love you." Beckett stroked a hand down her cheek. "We should tell the world."

Luna looked into his eyes. "You want to tell the whole world? You're definitely full of energy for someone as tired as you are."

"Okay then, we should get married to pledge it to each other."

"Would you love me more? No, because you already love me more than anybody ever in the history of the world loved someone." Luna put her finger on his lips. "Shh, it's true and you know it. I know it. That seems like enough." She grinned.

"I don't think this is funny. It is true. I love you. Don't make light of it. I seriously want to marry you."

"I'm sorry. It sounds so complicated. I just need convincing. What would we need to do to get married?"

"You'd need a dress. We'd plan a party. We have to apply for a license, the taxes. Also we'd need food and music, a guest list, invitations."

Luna asked, "So much! You Stiffnecks really like to turn something romantic into a big giant traffic jam. I'm exhausted just thinking about it. We'd do all of this before the baby comes?"

"Coming from someone who paddles ocean currents. Of course we'd do it before the baby comes, don't Waterfolk get married?"

Luna screwed up her face. "Not really, they just sort of pick someone and decide to travel with them."

Beckett rolled to his back with a huff. "I guess that is less complicated."

Luna curled up under his arm across his chest. "I don't mean to make it sound too simple, because if someone is choosing you, and you don't choose them it can shake up an entire family."

"Luna are you not choosing me?"

"Oh Beckett, I have chosen you, a million times over."

Beckett hugged her closer. "I choose you too. So let's have a big wedding and tell everyone."

Luna sighed dramatically. "Maybe we can talk about it later, when you've had a good sleep and a shower."

"Yeah, that sounds fair." He rubbed a finger up and down along her shoulder. "So explain it to me, Waterfolk just choose someone?"

"Yes, you bonk your paddleboard up to someone else's, and if they like you — it's simple."

"Just a bonk?"

"Yep. Like this . . ." Luna jumped to standing on the bed. "Hook your arm under your head. And lay back and smile up at me, like that. Now—"

Standing above him, jumping a little on the bed, Luna pretended to paddle while looking out on the horizon and then she glanced down. "Oh my, look at this hot guy with this nice smile floating here in the ocean. He even has a monarch tattoo on his arm, I think he might be the one I'll spend my whole life loving." Luna pretended to paddle closer. "Bonk."

"And that's all it takes—bonk?"

"That's all it takes. And then I climb over to your board just like this." She stepped a leg over him and dropped down onto his lap. "As long as your board is big enough."

Beckett laughed. "Oh you've seen my board."

Luna giggled. She took both of his hands in hers and pinned them up over his head. "You've been bonked, my love. Do you return it?"

Beckett looked up in her eyes. "You know I do."

"That's all we need. It's enough to go on. I promise."

Beckett nodded. "You're making sense, but also, you're naked, and you'll win because I can't think logically when you're naked." He pulled his hand from her grip and pushed the sheet that was between them down and pulled Luna's hips to his naked body. "Can we talk about it later, please?"

Luna kissed him sweetly. "Of course." And then she kissed down his shoulder to his chest and he stroked and caressed her thighs until just the proximity, the right-on-top-of-him, was enough to make him feel desperate. So she positioned herself, and he pulled her close and down and on, and they made love a second time that night in their bed, longer, slower, and taking their time.

At the end, Luna curled up under Beckett's arm and a second later he yawned loudly.

"You need more sleep."

"Just a little more. I'll get up soon."

Chapter 25

Hours later Beckett slowly climbed out of sleep to look around. The bed was warm, yet Luna's side was empty. Luna's side. They had spent the night together in a bed, with bedding. It had been comfortable and also unbelievable. Sleeping beside her had been so ordinary in a story that had been so extraordinary he had a nagging worry that it wouldn't-couldn't continue so normally.

But didn't Beckett have nagging feelings all the time? Fears and anxieties rattled around in his — where did Luna go? Was she eating breakfast? He checked the nightstand, his grandfather's watch lay there. He glanced at the time — 2:47. He stared at it for a while, trying to make sense of it. 2:47? That was pm. Most of a whole day gone. It was pouring rain outside. At least they would all be home.

He jerked up and pulled on his sweat pants, stretched, and headed straight for the bathroom. He looked much better, though too thin, too exhausted, but so much better than he imagined he must have looked yesterday, when he stumbled into the yard the first time, raging, or when he returned last night, soggy and worn completely out.

He took a piss, brushed his teeth and then, even though he was so hungry his stomach lining was threatening to eat his own liver, he jumped into the shower, because he supposed he owed it to everyone and also, warm water.

He might take five of these today. In the remaining five hours of today.

When he stepped out of the bathroom door, a little puppy attacked his ankles. He crouched down and it rolled over on its back and wiggled its feet in the air for pets and whimpered adoringly. He said, "Hello stranger, wonder when you started living in my home?"

He lumbered across the living room to the kitchen where the light was on. Dilly was washing dishes and dropped her dishtowel when he entered. "Beckett, good morning!"

Chickadee bustled around the counter to her laptop, flipped over a piece of paper, and shoved it under a pile. She tried to do it nonchalantly. She said, "Good morning!" With an exuberant brightness in her voice, but she couldn't cover it up, she was hiding something —

"What's on the paper Chickadee, are you planning presents for me?"

"Oh nothing, just paperwork—"

Luna stepped through the back door, soggy, wet through. She stomped her muddy boots and then sat to tug them off. "You're up! Good morning Sleepyhead."

"Good morning, babe." He moved across the kitchen to kiss her good morning. The puppy chewed on Beckett's ankles. Beckett turned back to Chickadee, "Something to do with the house, the land, or me?" Shark chomped down hard. Beckett asked, "Everyone can see this dog, right? It's not a figment of my imagination?"

Luna laughed. "That's Shark, Chickadee got him as a replacement when you didn't come home right away."

Beckett chuckled, looked down at the puppy growling at his foot. "It's cuter than me for sure."

Out of the corner of his eye he noticed Chickadee grab the stack of papers she had hidden earlier, put them under her arm and look around distracted. Then she seemed to notice Beckett watching her. "Beckett did you meet the puppy?"

Beckett squinted his eyes, "Yeah, and hey Chickadee, we should talk about all the things you've got to tell me about, huh?"

"Who us? Need to talk? No, um, but I do need to go see Roscoe about something." And with that Chickadee stalked out of the house.

Part Two:

The Deep

Chapter 26

Luna shoved her shoulder against the barn door, her arms full of trays of eggs. She spun around and — whoa — "Beckett?"

"Yeah?" He tucked a pencil behind his ear.

She deposited the tray on a shelf and leaned there, eyes squinted, looking him up and down. "You're in the middle of the barn wearing a tool belt. That is so hot."

Beckett looked down. "You think so? I mean I do have pants on too."

"Yep, pants, shirt, tool belt, pencil behind the ear, are you building something? Please be building something so I can watch. Hopefully, you aren't just standing here waiting for me to walk in. This is all new and oh so unexpected." She grinned.

"It is my house, I fix things. It's my tool belt."

"That makes sense, but when you were coming home, I could only imagine you coming through the door. Maybe in bed. Possibly leaning over the porch railing. The rest of the stuff, you actually working on the farm, building things, that's awesome. If I had known this, I would have gotten you out of bed days ago."

He grinned. "I could still use another day of sleep, but — have you noticed Chickadee is hiding something?"

"Is she? I hadn't noticed." She kicked off one of her rain boots with a grunt and tossed it to the side. "She seems the way she always does." She shoved off the other boot. "But then who can pay that much attention when Beckett is home and wearing a tool belt, like you are."

Beckett watched in amazement as Luna wiggled down her yoga pants and kicked them off. His eyes went wide. "What's this?"

She walked right up to him. "Me. Hormonal. You, hot. And all that." She grabbed the collar of his shirt and pulled him toward her for a kiss. "Your mouth feel better?"

"Much. And—" He wrapped his arms around her, lifted her off the ground, and carried her to the worktable. With one arm he shoved the assorted tools to the side, but seeing that there was sawdust everywhere, said, "Wait, just a minute," and put her down. He grabbed a towel and hurriedly swept the dust and splinters off the table and tossed the towel over his shoulder with a grin. "Okay now." He lifted her to the tool table. Luna worked on the top button of his pants and pushed them down from his body.

"And what?"

He kissed down her cheek to her ear. "And what, what?"

She giggled. "You said, 'Much, and...'"

His hands rubbed down her thigh pulling it up to his hip. "Was I saying something? You took your pants off earlier and—"

He unbuckled the tool belt, dropping it to the hay at his feet. "Sorry, that would be entirely ridiculous to wear during this." He kissed down her neck.

"I'm still wearing my raincoat." She was leaned back on her arms, big raincoat hiding the top half of her body, naked thighs wrapped around his body, pulling him closer.

He laughed. "Yep, you took off your pants *before* you took off your raincoat. Truly one of the most epic things about you."

"Really now? I'm a paddleboarder. I can travel for really long distances, and you're saying I'm epic because I took my pants off before my raincoat?" She hooked her feet behind his hips and teased him even closer, giggling.

"Right now it's easily one of the top three, but you know I can't count when you're—"

"When I'm what?" She rocked her hips against him.

"When — you—" He kissed the corner of her smiling lips and rushed to close the space between them. With his head tucked into her rubber-covered shoulder, her legs wrapped around, they moved and rocked and pushed, until he rose up, dazed, out of his head, bothered by the foreign smell of her raincoat — he unbuttoned the front and shoved it open and folded in on her now-uncovered body. Pulling her hips up and closer. His pushing became harder more desperate. He said, "Hold me."

She held on tighter around his shoulders.

"Hold me," he said again as he rocked and pushed against her body.

"I have you. It's okay," she said into his ear. "I have you."

His cheek rubbed against hers. "Don't let me go."

"I won't. I promise, Beckett. I promise."

He pushed into her more relentlessly, until finally at least he ended, and the pause was long, they stayed connected. His breathing ragged. Finally he kissed the soft place in front of her ear.

She stroked down his cheek and looked in his eyes. "You okay?"

"I was splintering apart."

"Oh Beckett how did we get from raincoats and tool belts to there?"

His body was heavy on her chest, his mouth on her shoulder, he shook his head. "I don't know. I think it was the nightmares I've been having, you know?"

She rubbed a soothing palm down the length of his back. "I know. Every night since you've been home."

"In them you're gone, or you're broken, or pieces, and I'm trying to hold you all together." His breathing was heavy. "In one I'm carrying you, like when I found you on the island after the storm, but your body is sand and you're sifting from my arms and I'm trying to hold you in one piece."

"So it's me that was splintering?"

He nodded quietly. "It was intense."

She rubbed her hands down his back and pulled him in tighter to her body. "I'm not splintering, you make me whole."

He kissed her slowly. "Good, because I mean to take care of you Luna, to keep you safe. No matter what."

"I know you do. You will."

"I will." He nodded looking into her eyes.

"Beckett, I hate to mention it, but your dream is actually becoming real—"

"What?"

She smiled up at him. "I think I may have a splinter in my ass."

"Oh, yeah, this is crazy uncomfortable." He straightened up, gave her a hand to pull her to sitting, and lifted her to the ground. "Though I'll admit I've never liked the barn this much in my life."

Luna said, "Me too. I love you. I can't believe you're home, and we can do this whenever—" Tears welled up in her eyes. She sobbed and then laughed, "There they are, the pregnancy moods."

He kissed her cheekbone tasting the salt. "I love you too. We should still get married."

She smiled. "Am I not bonking you enough?"

He laughed, picked up her hand, and kissed the knuckles.

"Your paddleboards look great, you patched them beautifully." He gestured to the wall where Luna's paddleboard and trailing paddleboard were freshly fixed and leaning.

"I patched Steve, there were some big dings from the storage. Boosy had to be reinforced, then re-glassed. Chickadee got me the materials from Heighton Port. I fixed the paddle too, but you saw that hanging on the wall of my room. I borrowed your tools."

"Did you wear my tool belt? Now that is hot." He kissed the tip of her nose.

"I couldn't, too round in the middle to hold it up. Sorry to ruin your fantasy. I have a lot of materials left over, so I was thinking I could make some boards. Dan wants one, and Rebecca."

Beckett pulled up his jeans, zipped them, and tossed Luna her pants. "Excellent idea. They want us to dinner, maybe this week?"

"I'd love that, I haven't gone anywhere in like forever."

Beckett's head jerked back, "Really? Why not?"

"We just figured it would be better. To wait."

"To hide you away? Whose idea was that?"

"I don't know, all of us, mine, without you here it felt weird to be pregnant at the grocery store, so I just didn't go." She wiggled into her pants.

"So today I'm patching the roof. Tonight we're having a family dinner because I have to get to the bottom of this Chickadee business. And tomorrow we're going out. Everywhere."

"By motorcycle? Please let it be by motorcycle." Her grin was wide.

Chapter 27

Beckett took a big bite full of chicken curry, the green kind, his favorite. He chewed it, smiled around the table, and very casually said, "So Chickadee, let me see your list."

"What list?"

"The list of things you need to talk to me about. There must be things going on. You met with Roscoe—"

Chickadee's eyes cut to Luna, "It's nothing, I'll handle it."

Beckett placed his napkin on the table and said, "As the man of the house—"

Chickadee countered with, "Holy crap, don't go pulling that bullshit with me. You'll start sounding like your Uncle Jimmy, and then we'll have nothing but mayhem and chaos."

Beckett laughed and put up his hands in surrender. "Okay, okay, let me start again. Chickadee, I'm home now. You've been taking care of me and the house for so long, but I'm home, I'm an adult, and I am in love, and I'm ready to hear the big things. I can take some of the weight off your shoulders." He smiled sweetly and batted his eyes. "Even though I know you're capable of doing it all."

Chickadee said, "It really is nothing, let's talk about something else."

Beckett said, "Okay, maybe you and Dilly can both weigh in on this, I asked Luna to marry me, and she said," his voice rose to a falsetto, "'that sounds like too much trouble.'"

Dilly clapped her hands, squealed, and grasped Luna's hand. "Trouble? No trouble at all, I can do everything, Luna. We can throw a big wedding in the garden, with lights and..." Her voice trailed off.

Beckett was watching Chickadee Intently. "What do you think Chickadee, big wedding in the garden?"

Chickadee said, "I think Luna is right, we should keep the trouble down to a minimum and—"

Beckett leaned forward. "Now you have to tell me. I can handle it. Let me know."

Chickadee scowled. "Dryden is causing trouble." She glanced around the table. "We should talk this over in private."

Beckett leaned back in his chair. "Dryden? What do you mean? What could she—"

Luna said, "I can go. I need to take Shark for a walk anyway, it's fine." She carried her dishes to the sink.

Beckett wanted to tell her not to go, but he was having trouble coming up with the words because his brain was whirring through possible explanations. What could Dryden want with him?

Dilly said, "Luna I'll come with you to let Beckett and Chickie talk."

They both left the room and Beckett stared dumbfounded at Chickadee. "What the hell?"

Chickadee sighed, pulled a stack of papers from a pile near her laptop, and placed them on the table with a smack. She banged her hand down on top.

"When you were missing I went to see Dryden and her family to ask if they had heard from you."

"Why would—"

"Dryden told Luna that you were communicating with her, and that you had never mentioned Luna. I knew it was bullshit, but also, I couldn't think of what else to do."

Beckett ran his hand over his head through his scraggly hair. "She said that? Luna must have been frantic."

"Dilly and I did the best we could, but you know, and that's not the worst of it."

"But wait, doesn't Dryden have a guy, what's his name, the Conner kid?"

"Joshua Conner died, front lines in the East, about three months before you were sent to the Outpost."

"Oh."

"Yeah, oh."

"Dryden thinks she can have me back?"

"It's worse than that my dear. She has a contract."

Beckett shook his head as if in a daze. "What are you talking about Chickadee?"

"Now I want you to stay calm. Deep breaths, okay? We're going to work through this."

"Chickadee."

"When I went there to ask if they knew anything from you, Dryden's mother said that it was strange they hadn't heard from you since you and Dryden were going to be married. I told her that was a perfectly piece-of-horseshit thing to say and she said there was a contract, to wed you two, but also, and perhaps more complicated, because Luna is right, marriage is complicated — giving most of your everything to that asinine family."

Beckett continued to shake his head. "A contract? What contract? I never signed a contract, what?"

"Consider it your Uncle Jimmy's farewell fuck you."

Beckett dropped his forehead to the table top and banged it there a couple of times. "Uncle Jimmy?"

"I can only assume he was out of his head at the time."

"But this is my house, my land—Luna."

"I know. Aunt Chickadee is trying to figure it out. That's why Roscoe is involved."

"Dryden wants half of everything?"

"Plus you."

Beckett pressed his thumbs to his lips thinking. "I need to go talk to her."

"We have a meeting set up, me and Roscoe — you, if you feel like it will help, with Dryden, her father, and her lawyer."

"So she lawyered up too? I'm going to go talk to her tomorrow." Beckett stood, shoving his chair back, and made to walk out of the room.

He came back a half second later. "If I hadn't asked, when were you planning to tell me that I was supposed to marry Dryden?"

"I thought I'd go to the meeting first, then explain it."

"Now see Chickadee, this is exactly it, the problem. I'm twenty-two years old. This is my house, my land. I want to marry Luna, and I'm going to have a child. You have to stop protecting me from bad news."

"But you know how you get dear."

"I know. I panic. I do stupid shit. But I'm trying to be better. Luna makes me better. Let me try that's all I ask." He started to leave then turned again. "What if we started hiding things from you because you sink sometimes? You would hate it because it's not fair."

Chickadee nodded. "I want to take care of you, that's all I've ever done."

Beckett slid down into the seat beside Chickadee, threw an arm around her shoulders and held her hand with the other. He kissed her cheek. "I know Chickadee. I love you. Thank you for handling this and everything. I want to come to the meeting. And I'm going to talk to Dryden, maybe we won't need a meeting at all. I'm sure once I explain she'll see."

That night, after piling on the couch and watching Chickadee's shows, including one that her friend Peter had produced, and laughing uproariously, Luna and Beckett brushed their teeth side by side in front of the bathroom mirror, put on pajamas, and climbed into bed together. They still slept in Luna's room, having decided that they liked it best.

Luna curled up under Beckett's arm. "Love, is there anything you need to talk to me about?"

Beckett considered for a second. He had been going over and over this all night. Should he tell Luna about Dryden? No, because she would worry, and he was going to fix it all tomorrow, anyway. But also, that was exactly like Chickadee, and so yes, he would tell her. And then at times he thought, "Why should I? She doesn't want to marry me, she hasn't a legal right to worry or know," and then he told himself that he was an asshole, that Luna was having his baby, and the baby would inherit all of this whether Luna married him or not and then...

But then he looked down into Luna's eyes, and she looked up at him, and he forgot all the arguments against telling her. "I've been thinking about distance tonight. How someone can be right here, but also distant. Like on the Outpost, when you were paddling away, all I could do was try to grab your board to keep you there, but I didn't know why. Why anything. Why you were leaving. Why I wanted you to stay. Why it was all so important, like forever important. Because we didn't tell each other anything, not really, and you left anyway." He pushed a piece of her loose hair behind her ear.

"You broke my heart when I saw you paddling the wrong way. And I didn't know why. You had been right there, but there was this huge distance between us."

Luna twirled her fingers, tracing circles on his chest. "Sometimes I think it's easier to communicate through the Monarch Constellation than up close."

Beckett pulled her chin up to look in her face. "Exactly love. It's hard to tell each other things face to face. Because it's easier to keep it secret and not cause pain. But also, knowing that distance is there, is too painful. So it's time to start facing each other. Telling the truth. You know?"

Luna nodded. Tears were eddying on the side of her nose spilling over onto his chest.

He said, "I have to tell you about something, but I want you to know I have this all under control—God, I sound just like Chickadee."

Luna laugh sobbed. "You do, you really do."

He kissed the top of her head. "I'm going to try to sound like Beckett instead, here goes — Luna, you've met Dryden?"

Luna's head shot up. She scrutinized his face. "Yes, I met her at the poetry slam."

"She seems to believe that she and I are going to be married. That she's got a contract. That she is part owner of my land."

Luna watched his face and couldn't think of a thing to say except, "Oh."

"Chickadee has involved Roscoe. This shouldn't be any problem for him, but while it gets sorted out, I think Dryden is going to be talked about a lot, and I want you to know that there's nothing for you to worry about."

Luna tucked her head back down to his chest. "She's in the photo on your dresser in your room."

"Oh, yeah, right. I haven't even gone in there since I got home. In the morning I'll clean up. Maybe we can turn my old room into the nursery."

Luna raised her head again. "We don't need a nursery, the baby is going to sleep right here."

Beckett looked down at the space between them, full of Luna's rounded tummy. He placed his hand on her stomach to feel again the now almost familiar pitch and roll.

Beckett smiled as the baby kicked. "

To be clear—you're pregnant?"

"Very." She tucked her head again, it was so much easier to talk of these things without looking into Beckett's eyes. "Beckett, did you love her?"

"I did. I was sixteen and I thought she was awesome. But she broke my heart. Not the way you did by paddling away, but by deciding she liked someone else. And it hurt and was awful for a while, but I got over her. Just because she was first doesn't make it important at all."

"Did you ask her to marry you?"

"I did. When I was sixteen, right before I went into the army. But the contract was my Uncle Jimmy's doing, and—" Beckett's fingers stroked up and down on her arm. "It will take some legal finagling to sort through it all."

Luna raised her head, frowning, a tear rolled down her nose, dropping to his chest. "It sounds really complicated."

100

He said, "It is, it will be, but I'll figure it out. I'm going to talk to her tomorrow. Maybe we won't even need to involve the lawyers."

Luna tucked her head into his chest again and nodded. "Yes, you should talk to her."

She sobbed and tears poured down her face and her shoulders shook with her tears.

"Are you crying? I'm so sorry. I don't want you to worry, I promise I can fix this."

Luna said, "It's just that's been my reason for not marrying you, complications, and here you are complicated with another girl."

"Yeah," Beckett kissed the top of her head. "Yeah, I know."

Chapter 28

Beckett was enjoying the day to day with Luna. Her laugh was beautiful, like it sparked, and maybe he didn't know that before. Watching Chickadee's favorite sitcoms last night, Luna had laughed at every joke, even the lame ones. Or especially the lame ones. Chickadee had nudged Beckett. "Watch her."

And he had. Luna giggling, sparkling and carefree. Her laugh had traveled through Dilly to Chickadee and then Beckett had stopped watching and had gotten caught up in it.

But today he didn't have time for laughing. He had to go to Dryden's house and talk some sense into her.

Luna followed Beckett to the truck, a raincoat over her head. He climbed in and rolled the window down to say goodbye.

Luna said, "Take deep breaths. It's only a contract."

"Contracts are usually pretty serious though."

She grinned, rivers of rain rolling down her hood. "Not when Roscoe is around."

"True. You should get in the house, it's way too wet out here."

"A little water never hurt anyone. Just don't try and figure anything out or worry too much. We'll get through this, whatever it is." The rain poured around them.

Beckett leaned his temple on the steering wheel. "I'm kind of tired of just getting through though. I'd like to figure something out before it's a crisis for once."

Luna nodded. "Yeah, I know. So that's why I'm amending that thing I just said — when in doubt, panic."

"Panic?"

"Yep, throw a leg over the railing of your ship and bellyflop."

"How will that help?"

"Element of surprise. You bellyflop in front of a girl and she'll do anything you ask."

"Really?"

"Worked for me." Luna leaned in to kiss Beckett on the dimple right beside his smile, and the small lake that had formed on top of her hood dumped into his lap. "Oops!"

Beckett chuckled. She patted the truck door, "I'll see you when you get back!" spun around, and splashed away up the stairs to the porch, giggling the whole time.

Her giggles rang through his head as he drove the truck down the mountain and pulled into Dryden's driveway. The rain didn't seem like it would ever stop, maybe not ever, and it was getting on his last nerve. What he wanted to do was take Luna for a walk around the land showing her the West Forest and the Highland Trail and especially Bug Boulder. Beckett had found it and named it when he was seven years old because it looked like a big giant June Bug. When he was little Beckett would sit on it, sometimes he would pretend to ride it, and when his Uncle Jimmy had been on one of his terrorizing rampages Beckett would escape to the boulder and would stay there, sometimes overnight, until it was safe to go home.

Besides showing her around his land, he wanted to walk around the farmer's market with her, and the grocery store, and all his old haunts. He wanted to take her on the motorcycle, to Heighton Port to see Dan and Rebecca and Sarah.

Instead he was spending all the time in the house, in the barn, in bed. Out of the rain.

Bed was epic though.

He climbed out of the truck, raced to the steps, and leaned his collapsed umbrella on the porch. He remembered where to put it, in the space that Dryden's mom had long ago designated the umbrella and galoshes place. He banged on the door.

A minute later Dryden's voice called, "Coming!" She opened the door with a whoosh. "Oh, Beckett!" She threw herself on his chest, not minding his sopping wet raincoat, locking her arms around his neck.

He backed up trying to extricate himself from her grip, "Hi Dryden — we should talk."

"I missed you so much, Beckett." She clutched him tighter. "I didn't think I would ever see you again. I was so worried." She avoided his eyes, swooped off his raincoat, and placed it on the hook reserved for guests, right beside his umbrella. She pulled him by the arm into the house. "Would you like something to eat, drink?" She disappeared into the kitchen.

"No thanks, I've had a big breakfast." The living room was just as Beckett remembered it, orderly and excessively decorated, like how Beckett imagined a mom would keep a living room. Now it looked uncomfortable, but growing up Beckett had thought it was perfect.

Dryden's twittering laugh came from the kitchen. "Well, I can't compete with Dilly's cooking but I aim to try." She swept back into the room with a tall glass of ice water and put it on the table in front of the couch. "I'm so glad you came Beckett, so so glad." She gestured for him to sit and plopped down beside him, curled her feet up, and grasped his hand. "I'm just so happy you're back." She pulled his hand to her lips, kissed the knuckle, and tucked it into her lap.

Beckett gingerly pulled his hand away, clapped it down on her knee in what he hoped was a friendly, yet not-romantic gesture.

"I guess you know why I'm here." He ran his fingers through his hair and tried to figure out where to rest his hand out of her reach. "Chickadee tells me there's a contract of some—"

"Oh good, you heard. Yes, there's some stupid stack of papers that my dad and your uncle signed months and months ago. I read it, of course. It's mostly boring legalese, but the point is: we get married and we share our estates. Our family benefits, of course, but all of that is just the extra. We can't let it distract us from what's important." She pressed closer, now a centimeter between her hand on his chest.

Beckett leaned away into the arm of the couch. "What's important?"

"Us, Beckie, me and you. Ultimately the contract is just, you know, like a prenuptial agreement, that's all."

"Me and you?"

Her hand touched down, the weight of her pressed on his chest. "Me and you. It's a legal document. But it's just about us getting married. And that part is easy, because we've been together since I was sixteen years old. And I know I'm not perfect, that I hurt you, but I was young, I didn't know what I wanted." Her fingers plucked at his shirt's fabric and rolled it between her fingers. "But I know now. There's a contract, and so it's easy. Me and you, together."

Beckett was so shocked, he had trouble mounting the defense the situation required. Like walking home from the war he lumbered into a catastrophe without a good plan or even a good response. "Um..." He scrambled for what to add.

"I know you might have complications. But, the contract is about more than just our marriage. It's about our families. Their safety. Since we've loved each other for so long it's awesome that we can be together, and we can help the people around us. It's the Universe's way of saying we're meant to be, I think. Don't you?"

Beckett, pinned on the couch, wanted up, but his brain had ceased functioning. His shoulder leading, he performed a shift and shimmy to standing.

Dryden's eyes squinted up at him in distrust. "Don't you?"

"Don't I what?" Beckett's brow furrowed.

"Think we are meant to be? The first time you asked me to marry you we were sixteen, now here we are, older, wiser, and our families support us. It's time to do it. Get married."

Beckett shook his head slowly from side to side. "Our families support us?"

"Yes, our families signed the contract. My dad and your Uncle Jimmy."

"My Uncle Jimmy was only family in name. You know this Dryden. And as you know, he was a drunken asshole. Mean as a snake. You know this, you saw the bruises, my scars. You know what it was like for me. I don't understand how you can talk about this contract so flippantly like it's a family blessing."

Dryden dropped her feet to the ground and sat up. "I'm sorry. I know he was awful, but there's this contract, and it's not my doings. I don't have anything to do with it.

106

It's with my dad, and so there's nothing I can do but accept it. Luckily I love you. I always have. So it's easy to think of it as a blessing. The one good thing your Uncle Jimmy did."

Beckett scrubbed his hands down his face. "You love me."

"I always have, and I always will."

"You've read the contract?"

"It's pretty basic — there's a bunch of stuff about land and taxes and the war effort. My brother's war levy would be paid. That's an extra part. But basically we share everything. But that's okay, right? Because we would once we were married, anyway. That's what you said, years ago." Dryden fluffed and smoothed a pillow as she spoke.

Beckett took a deep breath, trying to unclench his teeth. "Dryden, I'm not going to marry you. I have someone, that I love, that I intend to marry."

"That little nomad girl?" She flipped her hair over her shoulder.

"Yes."

Dryden flinched. "She can't be more than eighteen!"

"She's nineteen and that — that, is none of your business. Her name is Luna."

"I just assumed she was one of Aunt Chickadee's 'projects' or your Aunt Dilly's love interests,"

"My Aunt Dilly's...what the hell? Dryden—"

Dryden crossed her arms over her chest with a pout. "You can't be serious about her."

Red crept up Beckett's neck from his shirt collar. "I'm very serious about her, I love her."

"Well, you aren't allowed to. You and I have a contract that says you're to marry me. My father says so. My brother needs his taxes paid. So you need to act like a grownup and accept that your dalliance with this little nomad girl can't last." Dryden nervously adjusted the coasters on the coffee table and then looked up at him. "You want to marry a Nomad girl, give her half of everything you own, do you even know her?"

His anger was thudding in his ears. "I know her. I told you, I love her. I will marry her. I'm sorry you had to hear it this way, so suddenly, but this is what's happening." He dropped into a chair. "You know, when I went into the army you said you loved me, that you always would. But guess what? Then you stopped. You blew me off by letter. You were going to marry someone else—"

"I made a mistake, I'm sorry."

"But that's not how this works, and..." Beckett stared across the room searching for the words.

Dryden jumped up suddenly, rounded the coffee table, and dropped into his lap, pulling her long legs and awkward angles up, and folding into his un-welcoming arms. "Beckie, we loved each other. We can do this. We need to. Please don't, please." Her forehead butted against his neck. "Please, we're supposed to get married, you promised."

She kissed up his neck.

"I was sixteen."

She nibbled on his earlobe. "Beckie, you loved me. You will again."

"I can't." He held his hands up, out, not touching.

She continued to kiss and nibble on his neck, rubbing on his chest, but Beckett sat unresponsive.

After a minute she huffed, shoved herself up, and glowered over him. "I won't allow it Beckett. You can't have her."

"I don't see how you can say that. I love her. I promise you that. You don't want to marry me when I love someone else. You deserve better than that."

"You might love her, but you love your house more, your farm, your land, your woods, your Bug Boulder." Her forefinger punctuated the air as she listed the things he loved.

His eyes grew wide. "What are you saying?"

"I'm saying you can't have both."

Chapter 29

Beckett slammed through the front door of the house and angrily stripped his raincoat off, tossing it to the ground. Chickadee fluttered in from the kitchen, but at the look on Beckett's face pulled to a stop. "What did that girl say?"

"She said she'll hold me to the contract. Call Roscoe, tell him I want a copy to read. Where's Luna?"

"She's with Dilly, with the goats, there's a birth."

"Oh." He grabbed his raincoat, tugged his arms back into it, and slammed out the front door of the house.

By the time he made it to the goat pen he was wet through. It was coming down in cascades. He made out Dilly and Luna leaned against a fence under the only lean-to roof in the whole area and noted to himself: build more roofs, literally everywhere.

When he made it to the fence Luna, seeing the despair on his face, said, "Oh no."

"I don't know what I'm going to do, she's going to take it all."

Luna said, "Oh Beckett, love, I'm so sorry."

"It's like she hates me."

Dilly said, "Chickadee would say she does, that she's a terrible person, but I can imagine the pressure she's under. Her family is pushing her to make this match. They have a contract. She's caught in the middle. She believed she could strike a deal with you because of your past, but didn't count on you not taking the deal. She's probably very stuck."

"And my land is at stake." He scowled, rain dripping down his face. "It's always been my number one priority to protect it."

Luna gave him a small smile. "I'm so sorry that this is happening to you, but guess what?"

He raised his eyes. "What?"

"Jasmine is giving birth. Right now." She turned her focus to the goat standing in the middle of the pen.

Beckett leaned on the fence beside Luna, arms wrapped, Luna's head on his shoulder. They watched the goat, standing, breathing, waiting. The scent of the fresh hay and the rain mingled to smell fragrant and new. Expectant. Beckett felt his body relax, until when Luna looked up at him with a big smile, he found himself able to smile back.

She said, "I love you, it's all going to be okay."

"Thank you. I love you too." He pressed his lips to her hair and breathed in.

Chapter 30

Beckett dressed up: slacks, buttoned shirt, shiny shoes, jacket, this was a big meeting. His everything depended on it. He stood at the mirror tightening his tie while Luna stretched out on the bed watching. "God, you are the hottest Stiffneck I've ever seen."

Beckett said, "Thanks, I think? How many have you seen?"

"I've laid eyes on like thirty." Luna grinned. "But I've only laid one. Speaking of which—" She patted the mattress beside her.

Beckett groaned and then pantomimed being pulled to the bed and struggling away. "I just tied my tie."

"You also know you're getting ready too early because you're nervous." Luna pulled her shirt off over her head and tossed it to the floor.

"You know I can't argue when you're naked."

"I'm not totally naked yet." She jumped to standing on the bed, like she used to jump to standing on her board, and slowly, teasingly pushed her yoga pants down. She kicked them to the floor. "*Now* I'm naked. Plus it will be easier to negotiate contracts if you've been well-loved first. I mean, look at you, one girl takes off her clothes, and you can't even think straight."

"Not just any girl." Beckett unbuttoned his shirt forgetting his tie and tugging at it desperately.

Luna bounce walked to the end of the bed and kissed him sweetly while helping him loosen his tie and unbutton his shirt. Her breath was warm in his ear. "You smell really good."

"I'm wearing an aftershave that I—"

She unbuckled his pants while he wrapped an arm around her legs and pushed her top half back. Luna bounced down to the bed with a giggle.

Beckett crawled over her. "If my sixteen-year-old self could see this, you, here, in my bed, whenever, always..." He kissed down her collarbone to her breast and turned over to his back.

Luna climbed on top of him. "You like having me here?" She buried her face in his neck and inhaled the scent there.

"God yes, you're—"

"Right here?" She gathered him up, and in, deep, and with an exhale whispered, "Because I like being here."

"Being here — living here—" He raised her hips and lowered them again. "This is your home."

She nibbled on the tender spot under his jaw. "Yes, I like it." They shifted and rocked, his hands on her thighs, her hands on his chest, lost in their rhythm, serious, concentrating, lost —

There was a loud knock and Chickadee's voice through the door said, "Beckie, we should get going soon."

Luna giggled against Beckett's neck.

Beckett called, "Um, out in a minute, Chickadee. I'm almost ready."

Luna giggled again.

Luna closed her eyes, pressed her temple into the side of his cheek, and continued on — until finally, with a moan, they were through.

Luna lick-kissed the sweat on Beckett's upper lip.

He threw his arms around her back and pulled her close with a laugh. "I don't have time for a shower."

"If we were on paddleboards you could just roll to the side into the water. After checking for sharks of course."

"Here on land we have to take showers. We attend meetings with the sharks."

Luna stroked lightly down his cheek and through his hair. "Just listen. Try not to argue or get too angry, just try to understand. It's easier to negotiate if you understand what everyone wants."

"How did you learn that?"

"I spent a lot of time traveling in groups. A disagreement a day, and those were the good days." Luna rolled off and stepped to the floor. Beckett watched her pull clothes over her sleek skin. She was still so beautiful, muscular and soft, angled and round. He grasped her hand and pulled her closer and rested his cheek on her rounded stomach.

"My number one priority is to keep the land, the house, for you and the baby. It's everything."

Luna wrapped her arms around his head and kissed the top of his head. "You have to get dressed my love."

Ten minutes later Beckett was bustling across the porch to the truck. Chickadee was already idling the engine, waiting. When he stepped out from under the porch roof, he glanced up. "No rain, so that's good."

Luna glanced up at the sky. "A storm is coming."

"Really?" Beckett looked from the sky to the truck. Suddenly leaving seemed like a big deal. "When, later tonight? Is it going to be a big storm." His hand paused on the truck door. "You'll be okay?"

Luna nodded. "Yeah, it will be — sure, I'll be okay."

"Are you sure, I know how storms upset you, and I don't —"

Chickadee rolled down the window. "We have to go dear, these contracts won't dissolve themselves."

Luna said, "It probably won't be too bad…"

"Well you don't have to worry, because I'll be back before it starts." Beckett wrenched open the door.

"Promise?"

"I promise, before the storm. Do I look okay?"

Luna leaned close. "You look better than before, you look rumpled, well-sexed, and happy. So that's good."

"Yeah that's good." He slid into the seat beside Dilly. "I'll be back, by dinner."

"No worries, I've got this, like always."

"Sure, and you say that a lot, but you don't always. I'll be back before the storm." Chickadee drove the truck away down the gravel drive.

Luna looked down at Shark, pulling at his leash toward the departing tail lights. "What are you going to do, chase it? Jump in the back?"

Shark looked at her head cocked.

Luna said, "I agree little guy, in my whole life I never saw people that leave so much."

She knelt down and frisked the puppy behind the ears. "Apparently it's something we have to get used to as land-based mammals. Waving goodbye."

Chapter 31

Beckett scanned around the table. Dryden was sitting beside her father and their lawyer. Beckett had Chickadee to his right, Roscoe, and Dilly, looking like she wished she hadn't come.

Dryden's face was set, her eyes glaring.

Her father introduced his lawyer, a Mr Peterson. They had brought a large imposing stack of papers.

Beckett hadn't been able to look at the contract yet, but Roscoe had said, enigmatically, "You're glad you haven't. You would be furious. Let me handle some of the big things, and we'll go through it line by line."

Roscoe spoke first. "I'm glad everyone could make it today. If you need a drink, help yourself." He gestured to the end of the table where there was a pitcher of ice water and a stack of cups.

Roscoe cleared his throat and began. "I've invited Beckett here today, as this contract names him the property owner. Also it reads like an agreement between Beckett and Dryden though Beckett was not present at the signing. Were you present, Dryden?"

She glanced at her lawyer before she spoke. "I wasn't."

"Did you know of the contents or intents before the contract was signed?"

Dryden looked down at her hands. "I did not."

Roscoe nodded slowly. It was as if in his head he was saying yes, yes, yes. "Beckett do you have any intention to marry Ms Dryden Jones at present or in the future?"

Beckett shook his head. "No, no intention."

"Dryden, do you have any intention to marry Beckett Stanford? I ask this because I think we can take the prenuptial part of this contract and argue it separately from the property aspects. It will be easier I think."

Dryden said, "I do."

Chickadee interrupted, "Do what — have intention to marry Beckie, are you kidding me?"

Dryden leveled her gaze at Beckett. "I have a promise and a contract, so yes, I intend to marry Beckett."

Roscoe said, "Okay then, we'll start with the beginning of the contract, page one." He flipped open a bulky folder.

Dryden's father, Ted, said, "I also brought this, the minutes of the last meeting of the Buckhorn Mountain and Charlesville Adjacent Unincorporated Farm Community Council. Before Jimmy Stanford passed away. My condolences again Chickadee, Beckett."

Chickadee imperiously straightened her spine. "None necessary, we're glad to be rid of the no good son of a —"

Roscoe said, "Chickadee," and she bit her lips together.

Ted continued, "At that meeting we decided on many new ordinances and guidelines. I'm sure Beckett, as the property owner, will want to read over them." He pushed a small stack of papers toward Beckett.

While everyone waited and seemed to be watching him, Beckett scanned down the first page, classic minute stuff, then the second page. His skimming stopped cold at the words: "To protect and secure the land of Buck-horn Mountain and the surrounding Charlesville Adjacent Farm Community from the immigration of refugees, migrants, Nomadic Water People, and other homeless and destitute peoples."

And there were paragraphs titled: Patrols. Gates. And finally: Arms.

Beckett rotated the papers toward Chickadee and tapped those paragraphs. She scowled.

Beckett asked Dryden, "Is this meant to intimidate me?"

Her father interjected, "Not at all Beckett." His smile was meant to be kind but couldn't mask his malice. "We simply want you to know what laws have been enacted. Besides that, a law prohibiting the migration to our village of refugees has nothing to do with you, right?" He raised his brows in inquiry.

Beckett scowled.

Roscoe said, "We're getting off topic."

"Excuse me Roscoe, but," Beckett turned to Dryden's father, "I'm seeing this for the first time. There are armed patrols?"

"Yes, the gates will be built at the end of the month. We have a sizable group of young men and women who have been hired to handle our protection. It's all here in the paperwork. The arms are bought and are stored at Village Hall."

Beckett asked, "Laws have been passed?"

"Oh yes, marriage contracts, land contracts, we had to collect a new protection tax. You'll see when you read the minutes. Your Uncle Jimmy was very vocal about saving the land for his nephew and his eventual family." Dryden's father gave a small nod and smile to his daughter.

Beckett's chest began to constrict, his breaths were becoming irregular, his panic rising.

Dryden's father continued, "Ultimately we want to keep the mountain for those that are born and bred on the mountain. We don't want to lose our land to an influx of people who don't belong here."

Beckett shoved his chair back away from the table. He was close to springing across the table aimed at Dryden's father's neck, a man who he never really cared for. He also considered racing for the door, the truck, and going home.

Instead he sat, hands on knees, staring at the ground, thinking for a minute, trying to get the better of the meaning of the words.

Luna had said to listen.

He tried to think that all through.

It sounded like there were laws forbidding his marriage to Luna.

Laws forbidding even her living there.

There were laws that his fucking Uncle Jimmy wrote that made it so that Beckett's child wouldn't get to call the mountain home.

There were armed patrols whose entire point was to keep people like Luna off the mountain.

He was going to be mired in this bullshit for fucking forever.

But his brain tripped on something Dryden's father had said. "You mentioned young men had been hired?"

"From the village, sons and nephews, some daughters, from the town."

Beckett scrubbed his hands down his face. "Why aren't they off fighting or placing sandbags?"

Dryden's father put his hand on the contract in front of him. "That's what this lays out. We, as a family, will be paying off their service contracts with tracts of land."

"My land?"

"In effect."

Beckett stood. He spoke directly to Chickadee. "I didn't even pay off my own service contract. I performed my duty to keep the land. For six years."

Chickadee said, "I know dear. Don't we know, Roscoe?"

"We haven't even started on this contract yet, Beckett," said Roscoe as he straightened the papers in front of him. "Let's begin."

Beckett glanced at the stack of papers that looked innocuous enough, but threatened to take every bit of land, happiness, strength he had. "I need a moment, please." Beckett stood and left for the bathroom.

Chapter 32

"First, Sharky, we have to understand that—" Luna opened the refrigerator and pulled out the bag of bacon chips they kept for puppy training.

Shark bit Luna's foot.

Luna shoved her away, told her to sit, and gave her a treat. "Good Shark, so good. First thing to know is this: when land-dwellers tell you they'll give you a home, they literally mean a house to live in. In one place. Sometimes they'll be there, a lot of times they won't. Sometimes you'll get to go other places too. But mostly you'll be expected to stay by yourself. You'll have to come up with things to do. That's the truth."

Shark jumped and barked wanting another treat. "Good Shark, good. They aren't big on sticking together these land-dwellers. That's important to understand. Want to watch TV?"

Luna scooped up the puppy, plopped on the couch, and picked a show to watch.

The light in the room dimmed.

This was one of her favorite sitcoms. And she had already watched this episode three times. The main character pretended to be a table so the other characters would divulge their secrets. She didn't look anything like a table, but that was the whole point. She was a terrible table, yet no one noticed. Luna usually laughed hysterically, but this time she was too distracted to find it funny.

When the main actress said, "Aha!" and revealed herself under the tablecloth, instead of laughing, Luna continued speaking to Shark. "But more importantly you should to know this—the land is the number one priority."

Luna's back was to the window. She tried to ignore the ominous sky, but the room was darkening, dangerously. She pulled Shark to her chest and rubbed her face in the puppy's ruff as the storm clouds moved in.

Chapter 33

Beckett returned from the bathroom and slumped into his chair with a gruff apology directed at Roscoe.

"We're perusing Section 2: Addendum 39." Roscoe passed Beckett a sheet of paper.

Dryden's father said, "I'm not sure why we're even discussing this. We only need to begin implementation. Most of the plans are already in motion. And Beckett, a breach of contract affects too many lives."

Roscoe pointedly said, "Now Ted, Beckett hasn't even had a moment to read this, or to confer with me, so why don't we give him a break."

Beckett's eyes shot to the window as an arc of lightning lit up the sky with a sizzling closeness and a kaboom that shook the window's pane. What Beckett hadn't been noticing, that the sky had darkened, that storm clouds had moved in, and that while he had been in the bathroom Roscoe had turned on lights so they could read, suddenly became evident.

"Oh crap!" He jumped from his chair. "Oh man, I have to go home. Chickadee can you handle this?"

"Oh, yes dearest, certainly. Roscoe, can you give Dilly and me a ride home?" She yanked the keys from her pocket and passed them to Beckett without waiting for Roscoe's answer.

"Okay, I have to go." Beckett absentmindedly patted his pocket for the keys that were in his hand. "Roscoe can you make sure I have a copy of the contract?"

Roscoe nodded. "I'll bring it when I drive Chickadee and Dilly home."

"Good, thanks." Beckett rushed for the front door, crossed the porch, and sprinted through the rain to the truck. As he reversed out of Roscoe's driveway, he dialed Luna, and set it for speaker. The phone rang and rang.

"Come on Luna. Come on."

She didn't answer.

He hooked the steering wheel left, headed up mountain drive, and dialed her number again. It rang and rang and finally her voice answered. "Hello?"

"I'm coming home, I'm—" An arc of a lightning bolt flashed across the sky. There was a loud boom. Luna made a noise like a whimper.

"I'm nine minutes away, where are you right now?"

"Kitchen."

"Okay, good." At a stop sign Beckett gunned the engine and hydroplaned for a second. "Now I'm seven and a half minutes away. How's the storm there?"

"Terrible, loud. Nothing I can't handle, of course."

"Of course. Look, I know I promised I'd be back in time, but I was — I lost focus for a second, it snuck up on me."

"It's okay—" Three distinct flashes of light interrupted her and an epically large boom crash. "Please come."

"I'm at the intersection with Route 33, at a red light." Beckett drummed his hands impatiently on the dashboard. "Green. Straight shot home, I'll see you in five minutes. No worries, right?" He sped up the curving mountain road. "What have you been doing while I was gone?"

"I was watching The Queen of Everything."

"The scene where she's a table?" Beckett braked for a light and revved his engine impatiently.

"Yes."

"It's funny because she doesn't look like a table."

Lightning lit up the sky.

"Can you come Beckett, please?"

"I'm almost there. Just — don't be scared okay? I'm almost there."

Beckett swung the truck up to the porch, jumped out, and splashed up the steps. He yanked open the door. "Luna!" He rushed to the kitchen and found her cross-legged under the table with Shark in her lap.

He leaned down and smiled. "Hey babe."

"Hey you."

"Got room for me?" He swung himself down, under, and cross-legged right in front of Luna knee to knee.

Even sitting he had to bend forward because of his height. He cocked his head to inspect the underside of the table, "This is a view I've never taken before."

"Shark seemed really scared, so I thought we'd sit here."

"Well, that makes sense." Beckett rubbed Shark all around the scruff of his neck. "No one wants a scared puppy." Shark flipped to her back and wiggled her paws begging for belly rubs.

Luna asked, "Did you accomplish anything?"

"Nope not a thing. It's far more sucky than I thought, and I may have made it even worse."

Lightning flashed, they both ducked their heads in anticipation of the boom. Boom! The room was dark, the rain loud.

"You didn't solve anything?"

"I left before it even started."

"Oh. For me?"

"Of course for you. But Shark too, I couldn't leave Shark alone here during a storm, I promised him." Beckett smiled and Luna leaned forward, her head on his shoulder, his arms around.

Chapter 34

The next morning surprisingly Beckett was up first bouncing the edge of the bed. "Hey, sleepyhead, hey, wake up."

Luna startled awake from a deep sleep. She was surrounded by a wall of pillows, one behind her back, one between her legs, one beside her stomach, one under her head. She looked up, creases across her cheeks.

"You're sleeping deep and late and something cool is happening."

Luna smacked her lips groggily. "No rain?"

Beckett acted incredulous. "How do you know that, you literally just woke up?"

She grinned. "I can smell the north wind, plus the constellations, also the currents. And there's a block of sun on the wall right past your head."

Beckett looked behind him. "Yes, sun! Sun, Luna. The rainy season has ended. Officially. Today. So I have made plans."

"What kind of plans, going somewhere?"

"Yes, you're going to load your paddleboard into the truck, and we're going to go to Heighton Port and you can go for a spin, and then we have been invited to Dan's for dinner and even more, but I'm not telling you until later because it's a surprise."

Luna bounced up. Her feet hit the floor, and she raced for the bathroom. "I'll be ready in three minutes." She returned a second later, holding her toothbrush. "Thank you."

"You're welcome. Now get ready. I'm packing some breakfast for the ride." He disappeared down the hall to the kitchen.

———————

Thirty minutes later they were in the truck driving away from the house. Luna took a big bite of hard-boiled egg, chewed, and swallowed. "I'm disappointed that we aren't on your motorcycle."

Beckett grinned. "You, my love, have lost the proportions necessary for being a rider. Specifically your belly is too big and your arms too short."

She playfully slapped him on the shoulder. "You could have just said my paddleboard wouldn't fit."

"Oh no, I promised I could make that fit. It's totally your belly. It behooves me to say you're gigantic now."

"This is going to be a big baby. I might also be giving birth to some cookies too." Luna patted her stomach. "The baby kicked."

Beckett put out his hand and Luna placed it in the spot on her tummy. "There."

They rode for a while in comfortable companionable silence as the truck snaked its way through traffic down the mountain. They passed a newly built but still empty guardhouse.

Beckett craned his neck looking at it as they drove by. "That's new. Part of the security program, I suppose."

Luna said, "Thank you for this, you have a lot going on, I'm glad you could take some time."

"My next meeting is tomorrow. While you're out on the ocean, I'll read the contract. No worries."

"I'd like to read it too. Just to know."

Beckett glanced at her over his driving arm. "Yeah. You should. I mean it when I say it's your land too, it's complicated right now, but I mean that."

"I know."

Chapter 35

Beckett pulled the truck up to the Heighton Port boat launch and Dan, Sarah, and Rebecca were waiting on the dock.

Dan yelled, "Hullo! The mountain folk descended to the coast for some fun and partying finally!" He hugged Beckett and then Luna. "Jeez, Luna, what did you eat?"

Sarah and Rebecca hugged everyone too, while Luna responded, "I'm pregnant, Dan."

"Oh really? You sure? I was thinking lack of exercise." He laughed heartily. "With all seriousness though, how far do you think you'll go today?"

Luna tossed her hair. "I'm going to keep it cool, like twelve miles, something like that."

"Yeah, keep it cool. While you do, I'm going to keep Beckett company. Sarah and Rebecca need to go into the office. They wanted to say welcome and see you off."

Rebecca said, "We're working on a new grant proposal. Another trip in September, wanna go, Beckett, Luna?"

Beckett counted on his fingers. "I think baby will be about a week old. What do you think Luna?"

Luna placed her paddle on the ground and turned to strap water and snacks to the board. "Babies really shouldn't be out on the high seas until they're at least two weeks old, so maybe next trip."

Sarah said, "It's so good seeing you both, together. Happy. We'll see you at dinner, our house, and then dancing!"

Luna turned to Beckett with excitement. "What, dancing?"

"That was the surprise."

"Awesome." She lifted her paddleboard up, Beckett grabbed the other end, and they hefted it to the end of the dock and lowered it to the water. Luna dropped to sitting on the dock with her foot out holding the board. She grabbed her paddle. "Okay, I'll see you in—"

"I almost forgot." Beckett unclasped his great grandfather's watch and fastened it around Luna's wrist. "What time will you be back?"

"Four. Sound good?"

"I'll be here."

She crouched and stepped to the paddleboard and deftly stood, barely rocking. Then she waved goodbye and set off for the day.

Chapter 36

Dan stood beside Beckett watching her go. "Doing better Army? I haven't seen you since, you know, you were a half-crazed belligerent asshat."

Beckett said, "Yeah, about that. Did I say I was sorry?"

"Yes, but more is good. No worries though, really. When I returned home from the Navy I hit the bars, got stupid drunk, and fought the sidewalk with my face. And I had nothing and nobody to deal with. Definitely not a baby on the way. Luna looks great."

"She's doing really great. It's dawning on me that this whole baby thing is actually happening. Want to ride with me?"

"Sure, Sarah just took my car." They climbed into the truck.

Dan asked, "What's the stack of official looking papers?"

"My marriage contract with a young woman named Dryden."

"Are you shitting me? The looker from your aunt's party? Phewie, does trouble follow you, or are you actively seeking it out? What does Luna think about this?"

"She's being supportive, but it sucks she has to even deal with it. I need to sit at your kitchen table and read over it if you don't mind."

"No problem. I can come up with something to do and we'll catch up later."

Chapter 37

Luna pushed her paddle in and down and through and counted her strokes and raced her shadow. And sprinted against her times. She circled a buoy, then decided to go farther, to a small Outpost, that would be a fun midway point. The sun was reaching its zenith and warmed her skin. She breathed in deeply, the smell of sweat and ocean and breeze. She felt real and alive for the first time in months.

While she paddled, she explained things to the baby. "Hello love, this is what your mama does. She paddles. She's a freaking ocean goddess, and if you tell her you want to go to the farthest islands, she'll say okay. She'll paddle you there. Like a superhero." Her paddle sliced through the water and propelled her forward.

"Your mama also can read the weather in the sky. She can predict three days away. Like right now, beautiful, but this afternoon an onshore wind will come up, just in time to push me back to land. I'll follow breeze and current, but I don't have to, because I can navigate by the stars too. I'll teach you how."

She counted strokes in her head, "One, two, three, four, five." Then switched sides. "One, two, three, four, five." She dragged her paddle, spinning in a quick circle, then plowed it down through the water again, propelling herself faster, faster, faster.

It took her two hours to get to the outpost, now just two inches of a top floor. With water lapping over the edge and sea lions on every square inch. She floated on her paddleboard nearby, feet dangling in the water, eating lunch, watching the birds circle overhead waiting for a crumb or two. "The thing is baby, we won't do this much. Not like me, growing up out here. Instead we'll be living on land. I'll need to find some badass things to do there. Like maybe learning to drive a motorcycle."

She ripped a piece of bread in two and chewed half of it slowly. "That would be fun." She lay there for a while enjoying the rhythm of the up and down of the water, lolling. Warm skin and after a long time she stood. "But here's the thing baby, the ocean is awesome, it's always been my home, and it's nothing to be afraid of, I promise. But your dad is on land. So that's where we're headed."

She pushed her paddle back and began the journey home.

Chapter 38

"Hey!"

Beckett waved his arms. "I missed you!"

She checked the watch. "Right on time!"

"I've been here for an hour already."

She pulled up to the dock, stepped onto it, and stretched her shoulders gingerly. "I'm going to be feeling that tomorrow."

"How far did you go?"

"About fifteen miles. Too far. But also, perfectly too far. It felt great."

Beckett lifted and shoved her board into the bed of his truck. "Ready to go get dinner?"

"Famished."

Chapter 39

Dan had cooked chili. With cornbread and a salad. Everyone served themselves buffet style because he was, "Not going to wait on you hand and foot because this was not a ship."

They all sat around the table, in an assortment of chairs, eating, and laughing. Dan asked Luna all about her day and she regaled them with stories. The buoy, the dolphins, a seal, and there had been a big container ship headed to port that Luna had circled to prove she could.

"Those things move at a fast clip." Dan leaned forward elbows on the table hanging on her every word.

"Well, I was faster." Luna took a big bite of salad, swallowed it, and grinned. "For about twenty minutes. After it though I had to sit and rest for forty-five minutes. I'm a weakling."

Dan shook his head. "If you think about it Beckett is kind of like your kryptonite."

She giggled. "Then again, with his help I am creating a live human being, plus occasionally paddling fifteen miles. The case might be made for me getting even stronger." Beckett hugged her around the shoulders.

"So besides Ocean Goddess, you're a Mother Goddess. I'd like to mention that I made chili tonight, you're welcome." Everyone laughed.

Sarah said, "Dan is super excited about being Uncle Dan. It's most of what he thinks about."

"I'm trying to decide if the baby should call me Unkie Danny or Uncle Daniel. What kind of authority figure do I want to be?"

"Maybe you let Beckett be the authority figure, and you can be Unkie, and crack jokes all the time. It's what you're suited for, and that way baby will love you a lot." Sarah kissed him on the cheek and nuzzled into his shoulder.

"Yes, that's my strategy. Can I be godfather, too?"

Luna asked, "I mean, yes, of course, no one else is asking, but why don't you and Sarah have a baby, too?"

"Sadly, we can't afford to, the tax is too high." Dan kissed the top of Sarah's head.

"The tax?"

"It's the amount you have to pay the government to allow you to have a baby. It's a small fortune. Number one reason why you're the only pregnant lady for miles around."

"Oh." Luna turned to Beckett. "You never mentioned any tax."

"Oops man." Dan shrugged. "I didn't mean to get you in trouble."

"I just assumed Chickadee had told you." Beckett squeezed Luna's hand. "Apparently she paid the taxes the first month."

Luna sighed. "There are so many rules to living on land, I can't get used to it."

Sarah said, "Speaking of giant outlays of cash, Dan tells me you're having legal troubles, Beckett?"

"Yep. My insane and violent Uncle Jimmy saw fit to sign me contractually into a marriage while I was away on the Outpost."

Rebecca said, "Sorry, I phased out for a bit, too much talk about babies. Your uncle arranged a marriage for you?"

"And he died before I could kill him for it."

"Oh my god Beckett that's the worst." Sarah patted the back of Luna's hand with a frown.

Rebecca asked, "To who?"

Beckett said, "Some girl."

Luna said, "Dryden, that girl from Aunt Chickadee's party."

Rebecca pretended to jump from her chair. "Oh no she doesn't, I'm going to kick her ass."

Sarah laughed and shook her head. "Beckett, what are you going to do?"

"Roscoe is going to fight it. I'm pretending like that will work. But I was reading through the contract today and Uncle Jimmy gave away half of everything I own. I'm not sure I can get away without losing a lot."

"All that land, you could lose half of it?" Dan shook his head and pretended to wipe his eyes. "I was getting used to the idea that you were the richest guy around. Now you're only half as rich." He dramatically sighed.

"Want to hear the ironic part? I could have bought my way out of the service, but no, I wanted to save the land, the entire tract, all of it, intact." Beckett scowled. "It's my biggest priority."

Dan said, "Well it definitely needs to be."

Chapter 40

Luna yawned, in the middle of the dance floor, a big gaping yawn of epic proportions. Beckett grasped her hand, spun her to him, and said into her ear, loudly, over the music, "Do you need to go back?"

"Not yet. Three more dances."

Beckett grinned widely and spun her out and back in. "You've gotten really good at this."

"That's good because literally everyone is watching, It's like they've never seen a pregnant woman before."

Beckett scoped the room, the other dancers were giving them a wide berth. Nearly everyone was noticing, whispering, watching. Plus, since they arrived, everybody, from the doorman to the bartender, to the waitress, and many of the other club goers, asked, "Are you pregnant?" With follow up questions like, "How?" or, "For how long?" and, "Are you really going to have a baby?"

Luna answered with a smile and a yes and explanations to their concerns, but she had been doing that all night. Without much practice on land, in people, around Stiffnecks. While pregnant, plus dancing. "Many of them haven't seen a pregnant person before, or not up close and personal." Beckett kissed her temple. "Definitely not so effortlessly."

"Am I making this look effortless?" Luna wiggled her hips. "Because there's a lot of yawn stifling and mental counting for me to stay awake while dancing."

"I'll sit with you."

She said, "Three more."

A half hour later she and Beckett piled into the booth beside Sarah and Dan. Beckett asked, "Where's Rebecca?"

"Dancing with some cutie." Sarah pointed at the dance floor. "She'll probably be out much later tonight."

"Ah."

Luna put her head against Beckett's shoulder and curled her legs under herself.

"Luna, you look tired," said Dan, "but I have to dance a bit more before we go home."

She nodded and yawned as Dan and Sarah headed for the dance floor.

It took about two minutes before Beckett felt Luna go limp with sleep. She lolled forward, so he pulled her across his lap, draped on his chest, and held her while she slept. She was sleeping so deeply that she began to snore.

A while later Dan and Sarah returned. "Well, she's out."

"Sleeping like she's on land."

"Do you think you can wake her to go home?"

Beckett whispered, "Luna, wake up, Luna?" Her head lolled and she nestled in even more. "Okay then." Beckett wriggled out of the booth, pulled her up into his arms, and carried Luna out of the club to the car.

Chapter 41

The following morning Luna was beaming at Beckett from the passenger seat of the truck as they drove home from Heighton Port. "That was so much fun, everything, from the paddling, to seeing Sarah, Rebecca, and Dan again, to the club. That was awesome. If you want to surprise me like that again, you get to. Anytime."

Beckett smiled over his driving arm. "I wish we could have stayed for a leisurely breakfast, but I'm worried about traffic, and my meeting starts in..." He checked his watch. "Four hours."

"At least it's at your house this time."

"Yes, you're okay with staying clear? I just don't want to complicate the negotiation."

Luna turned and looked out the window, her face less animated than before. "Yeah."

"It's for ease. Dryden's dad is being pretty anti-migrant. I don't want him to—"

"Sure. I'll just read in my room."

They rode in silence for a few minutes. "How's baby doing this morning?"

"Kicking like crazy, here." She guided his palm to her lower belly.

"Wow." A bulge rolled from one side to the other. "You're really pregnant?"

"Truly."

"How does one take care of a baby, I wonder?"

Luna giggled. "I think it begins with a splash." She reached into the floorboards and pulled up a stack of books. "Also reading these books Dr Mags got for me."

"Read me some titles."

"Giving Birth, Baby's First Weeks, 1-2-3 Everything Baby. I guess by the time I read these I'll know what I'm doing."

"How long did you say we have?"

"About six weeks I think?"

"Six weeks. I've got to get this land thing taken care of. Argh."

Luna squinted her eyes appraising his expression. "This is an interesting thing about you that I'm learning."

"What's that?"

"You say one thing, but you mean another. Are all Stiffnecks like that?"

"What the—well first of all, I thought we determined that the term Stiffneck is derogatory, so I get to be called a land-based animal. It suits me better."

Luna raised her brow and half-joked, "If you're acting like a Stiffneck, you get called a Stiffneck."

"Enlighten me."

"You say, to everyone, that the land is your number one priority, but it's not true."

Beckett pulled the truck to a stoplight and looked at her. "What about that isn't true?"

"It's not your number one priority, ever."

"I'm not getting you. Of course it is, what else would it be?"

"Me. Your number one priority has been me. In everything. You make sure I'm okay, often at great expense to yourself. But that's the truth. Yet you won't admit it."

The light turned green. Beckett slowly followed the stream of cars. Traffic was terrible. They weren't even at the entrance to the highway yet. He was right to leave early.

Beckett's brow darkened. "Yes, I know, it's a failing."

Luna's eyebrow arched incredulously. "A failing? Putting me first?"

"It's a little boy move. I need to start behaving like a grownup, looking at the big picture, the end game. I'm going to be a father soon, and I have to be responsible."

Luna scrutinized the side of his face. "So saying that a piece of land is your first priority is growing up?"

"Yes, taking care of you and the baby. Having land is the most important thing. To keep you safe."

Luna watched the buildings and the sidewalk crowded with people as it slowly crept by the window, most of the pedestrians going faster than their truck. Luna thought about how if there was water here, she could paddle home quicker than this. And that there would be water here soon enough. She craned her head to see — they had risen about a foot over sea level. Would there be water here? The scientists measured the rise by inches but it filled in spaces by tides and storms.

And hadn't it been a long time since she thought of that, the water rise, because she had been on the mountain, safe, for six months. Safe. Because of Beckett.

Staring out the window she said, "Do you hear yourself? You said your first priority is the land because of me. It's still true. It doesn't make you a boy it makes you honest."

"Are you just trying to win this discussion, because I'm not sure what your point is. Fine, you're my priority. While I'm bickering with my neighbors and my former girlfriend over the contract for my land, I'll remember: it's not for the land, it's for Luna. Does that sound better?"

"My point is that Waterfolk think of the people around them as their priority and say so. Neighbors, former girlfriends, relatives, they all matter. Because lives are interconnected. You might have a distant cousin who travels with a different family, but if they're nearby, they become part of your priority. It's all about the relationships. You're saying the opposite. I find it interesting."

"Dryden's father can smell my weakness, use it to his advantage. It's not interesting, it makes me a failure." Beckett rubbed through his hair, elbow on the door.

"So from now on you'll be putting the land first and me second? How about the baby, Chickadee and Dilly? What about Dryden, you loved her once, is she on your list?"

"I don't get what you want me to say."

Luna nodded. "Yeah, I know. Can I read the contract?"

Chapter 42

All the way up the mountain, through the stop and go traffic, the cars parked on the side of the road, families milling around, cars broken down, people on foot — Luna read. It was a lot of legal language, some of it seemed senseless, like, why the provisions for the reading of the minutes at the community meetings, why was that in there? Literally, who cared? She tried to make sense of —

Beckett's phone rang.

He answered, holding it to his ear as he drove the car along a ten mile per hour creep up the road, bumper to bumper. "Miss me already, Dan? We just left."

Then he said, "Oh. Oh man. Oh god. When?"

Luna could hear Dan's voice, tiny coming through the phone, he sounded upset, she couldn't make out the words—

"Beckett?"

He glanced at her and continued listening to Dan. "Uh huh," and "I can't believe it..."

He turned to Luna and whispered, "Jeffrey."

Then he listened to more, for longer. "Yeah, man, it sucks."

Again, "I know," and then, "will you hug everyone for me? I wish I could come back, but — I'll call later, and man, tell Sarah and Rebecca I'm so sorry."

He hung up the phone and dropped it down to the seat beside him.

"Jeffrey?" Luna's eyes were wide, scared.

"He died on the front lines. God, that war."

Luna grasped his hand and held it, tears welled up in her eyes.

"I just — no one gets out alive."

Luna kissed his fingers, much like that day when his hands were hooked through the chain-link fence. The only contact across the divide. "I'm so sorry Beckett. So, so sorry."

"I didn't know him for that long, you know? He had been friends with Sarah and Rebecca for a really long time. Oh man, what is Dr Mags going to do? They were really close. This sucks."

Luna nodded, clasping his hand, listening, quietly crying.

"Jeez, Jeffrey?" Beckett pulled the truck to a stop behind a stream of cars, blaring their horns, heading away from the coast, stuck at another standstill. "I have this meeting. I have to put this out of my mind and deal with the meeting."

Chapter 43

Luna was lying on the bed in her room.

Beckett had been called to the meeting. Regretfully he went though he was upset about Jeffrey and in no mood.

She lay there listening to the voices of Dryden's party as they entered the house, greeting each other, shaking hands. Dryden's dad sounded like a pompous ass.

Dryden sounded upbeat and flirty.

Luna picked at the bed cover. She was in here against all her best judgement. Why?

Beckett loved her.

He wanted to marry her.

He told her that she owned half of everything he owned.

Plus they were having a baby. She dropped lower on the pillows and stared up at the ceiling. Her head felt dizzy, she was tired. And frankly scared.

This was all too much to sit quietly and alone while her future was discussed. She had things to add. She had read the contract.

She had opinions.

And Dryden was in her dining room negotiating her way into Beckett's life while Luna was sitting alone in a bedroom. Seething.

Was she trying to lose Beckett?

Because this was how that worked.

If a bonk can start a relationship what was Luna doing sitting back and letting Dryden bonk up to Beckett?

Sky would be outraged if she saw Luna sitting here.

Luna swept her feet off the bed as if she would — what?

The land was Beckett's number one priority. He truly believed that.

But it wasn't hers.

Her number one priority — Beckett. From the moment he had bellyflopped off the boat.

But he had said he needed her to stay here while he handled it. She sank back on the pillows again, staring up at the ceiling once more.

He was losing himself in this.

She remembered being cuddled up under his strong arms that night on the Outpost and even though she lied about her name, and about her family, even though, he had told her that she could move to his mountain. She had asked, "My whole family?" And he had said, "Yes, we'll figure that out." And he had meant it. Because Beckett had a heart as big as the ocean. She loved that about him.

He made her feel safe.

Secure. Because his love was big enough to protect her always, to rescue her, to doing anything she needed him to do.

Yet now, here, his number one priority was the land.

She lay staring at the ceiling thinking back and forth about whats and hows and priorities and necessities.

She thought about how Beckett was her whole wide world.

Everything.

And she was his everything, but he seemed somehow lost.

And when Beckett was lost he needed someone to find him.

And Luna was a navigator.

That echoed in her mind.

She was a navigator.

She had opinions—

From the other room she heard Dryden voice, sing-song and flirtatious. "Beckie Dearest, you know this is what you need to do."

Right then the baby kicked.

Luna sat up. She crossed the room to the mirror and glanced at herself. She swept her hair back and twisted to see herself from all directions. She had on a yoga top and pants, with a light sweeping coverup that was airy and gauzy and floated. She tied it round the middle to close it, because sometimes her belly button was endearing, but not today, because this was not—

She hadn't thought this through, but never mind.

Going.

She walked out the bedroom headed to the dining room to join the meeting.

Chapter 44

Beckett was asking about Section 4 Article 8 — the one that specifically called for a sharing of land. He was walking a thin line, trying to gulp down his upset over Jeffrey's death, trying to not offend or outrage his opponent, while also trying to win the argument.

He was one raw nerve, about close to breaking something. Possibly the wall.

He had no intention of marrying Dryden, she was the past, she had broken his heart.

Yet now she was vying for his money and land, in possession of a legal document that Roscoe called "valid." Even though Beckett's uncle hadn't actually owned the land. Even though Uncle Jimmy had been a violent lunatic. Even though he was probably drunk when he signed it. Even though.

Simpering Dryden was sitting across the table smiling sweetly while she did this.

Beckett dropped his head into his hands as he listened to Roscoe read about how a large portion of Beckett's land would be broken into pieces and partitioned off as payment on government levy payments for the people who would be working the security detail. Beckett shook his head and groaned.

He pressed his mouth into his thumbs and wished Luna could be there, to hold his hand, to smile. He could feel the baby. That usually worked to clear his mind of these stressful things.

Roscoe said, "So this provision looks pretty clear, it's the amount of land that we need to discuss."

Beckett said, "No I want to go through this line by line by line."

And that's when Dryden said, in that flirtatious and patronizing tone, what she said, causing Luna to leave her room and stalk across the living room to join them.

Chapter 45

Beckett's eyes were locked on Dryden, trying to come up with something to say besides, "Are you shitting me with this?" When the footsteps sounded behind him. From the looks on the faces of Dryden and her father and their lawyer, someone new and totally unexpected had entered the room.

Luna.

Beckett swung in his seat. She stood in the side door of the dining room, rounded belly entering first.

Before Dryden could close her shock-opened mouth, or her father could say, "Who in the world?" Luna said, "Excuse my intrusion, everyone. Roscoe, I was hoping to sit in on the meeting and ask a few questions."

Roscoe raised his eyebrows with a bemused look. "Certainly Luna, have you read the contract?"

"Yes, this morning."

Beckett didn't know what to do or say so he jumped up and lifted an empty chair that had been beside Dryden and slid it to his side of the table and offered it to Luna.

"Thank you," she said simply, without looking at him. She sat gracefully in the seat.

Dryden's mouth continued to open and close. Her father asked, "And who exactly is this?"

Before Beckett could answer, Luna said, "I'm Luna Saturniidae, Beckett's partner." She leveled her gaze at Dryden. "I believe we met at Dilly's poetry slam." Her hand went to her stomach.

Dryden eyes gloomed over. "I don't remember, but — by partner you mean?"

"Yes, partner."

"You'll need to be more clear, this is a business arrangement?"

"No, much more than that."

Dryden glared. She turned to Beckett. "Can you please explain this Beckett?"

Luna glanced at Beckett expectantly.

He began hesitatingly, "Um, this is Luna, she—"

"We," Luna gestured between herself and Beckett, "bonked."

Dryden shook her head slowly. "You bonked?"

Luna didn't feel like smiling, she felt frankly sick to her stomach, to walk in here uninvited and pretend to have it all under control. None of it made her happy, but she hid it, and grinned widely. "Oh boy did we, twice yesterday."

Luna cut her eyes at Chickadee who looked about to fall out of her chair. Dilly had her lips pressed between her teeth. Roscoe had the corner of his mouth curled up. Everyone seemed to be enjoying the show, except Beckett.

His eyes were wildly taking in all the faces. "Um, I think we've lost sight of the meeting's purpose. We should get back to the provisional clause on page..."

Dryden continued to glare at Luna. "And you're pregnant."

Luna nodded and watched Dryden work through the facts.

"With Beckie's baby?"

Luna nodded again.

"Why didn't you tell me Beckie?"

"I did." He dropped his pencil to the table and put his hands out palms up. "I told you that I loved Luna, and you were making a mistake thinking we were going to be together."

"But I didn't believe you. Those were just words you said, I didn't think you really meant them."

Beckett's brows drew down, and he scowled. "Why wouldn't you?"

He looked at Luna and shook his head.

Luna looked down at the table in front of her — perhaps she had miscalculated. She had thought this through. She had also walked in here without thinking. Both were true. "I know my presence is difficult. I just have a few questions. I'll ask them quickly."

"Absolutely Luna, ask away." Roscoe passed Luna a copy of the contract.

"In the last section there's a list." Luna flipped through pages to the end. "Here, a list of names. These are the young men and women who would be running Buckhorn Mountain's security detail. This first name shares your last name Dryden?"

Dryden looked uncomfortable to be expected to answer civilly. "He's my younger brother."

"It says here he's sixteen years old and will head to the front, at Burnside, in two months."

Dryden nodded.

Luna turned to Beckett. "That's how old you were, when you joined, right?"

"Yes, but I went to the coast. I had sandbag duty."

Luna returned to speaking to Dryden's side of the table. "So, if I'm not mistaken, the main purpose of this deal, is that there will be, from Beckett's land, acres to exchange for your brother's service?"

Dryden nodded again.

Her father said, "We'd prefer he work here at home, securing this community, than fighting in the East."

Luna watched him speak, but was drawing circles around the word: sixteen. Around and around and around. She nodded and glanced at the list again. "This next name, Fred Smithson, it says he's eighteen years old?"

Roscoe answered, "His older brother died in the East. Fred is headed in his stead to pay off their family's duty."

Luna turned to Beckett. "Do you know him?"

"I went to school with his brother." Beckett shook his head slowly. "I hadn't heard he had died."

"What about this young woman, Cindy Thomas?"

Chickadee said, "That's the dear niece of my friend from school, remember Todd, Roscoe?"

"I do Chickadee. She's all that's left of the family."

"That's just sad is what that is. It's unconscionable that the war is taking all these young people and killing them."

"Chickie, careful around the kids," said Dilly.

"Well, it's true, isn't it? There's barely any young left, and they have to fight the wars too? They should send the old coots to fight, like drunken Uncle Jimmy. Or you Roscoe."

Roscoe said, "Now if I went to war who would fight all your battles, Chickadee?"

"True, I'd have to volunteer in your stead, because I couldn't live without you. And who wants me in the war, I'm not at all up to fighting speed."

Luna glanced up to see Dryden with a tear rolling down her cheek.

Beckett leaned in and whispered to Luna. "You have a point?"

Luna didn't look at him. She said quietly, "Not yet," and then asked the table, "what about these names, James and Josh Irwin and Twill Jones, they're listed as twelve and thirteen years old."

Roscoe said, "The Irwins live at the bottom of the mountain, without any land and twin boys that will need to fight once they're of age. Twill Jones is an orphan."

Luna flipped the page. "If you don't mind I'd like to continue to read the names." She continued through the list one by one, asking for a story for every name. Asking Beckett if he knew the kid or the family and then moving to the next one. "Dune Mayweather?"

"He's twenty-three and volunteered to keep his brother from going."

"That's nice of him considering, huh?"

"Very nice."

Until she finally came to the bottom of the list. She silently counted the names, checking each with the pen. "That's thirty-three. Is that every young person that lives here on the mountain and in the community?"

Mr Peterson, Dryden's lawyer, said, "There are about forty-six young people in total. These are the ones for whom the service requirements would create a terrible strain on the family or would be impossible."

Luna said, "I need something else clarified, and it's hard to speak of, my apologies Dryden. We're assuming that to fight in the East is a death sentence? I mean, Beckett lost a friend yesterday, in the war."

Mr Peterson said, "The survival rate is very grim."

Dryden sniffled.

Luna looked down, her pen was still circling numbers on the page, nervously. "I would assume it would get worse too. The death rate I mean." She looked at Dryden's father. "These people would be willing to work as part of the community's security detail?"

"They're willing."

Luna flipped the pages of the contract back to the beginning. "So basically this contract combines your smaller tract of land with Beckett's larger tract of land and cedes it to the government in exchange for the lives of all these young people, then they will in turn protect the mountain."

Beckett groaned. "Baby, I see what you're getting at, but you have to understand—"

"That's why I'm asking, so I can understand."

Beckett leaned toward her speaking low. "You have to trust me, you don't understand this."

"I'm asking for the facts, so I can make my decision—

Beckett shoved his chair back and stood up. "Aargh." He ran his hands through his hair. He dropped his arms. "You need the facts, Luna? Okay, here they are. My Uncle Jimmy beat me. Sometimes daily." He turned to Roscoe. "You saw it, right? I'm not making this up."

"I did see it. You were covered in bruises. I called Chickadee and told her to come home."

"—And you got me a restraining order. You knew what he was capable of." He turned on Dryden and her father. "I was eight at the time. Eight. But also, because he was my legal guardian, we couldn't get him to leave. I slept outside, or in the barn." He spoke directly to Dryden. "I told you this, didn't I tell you this?"

She nodded.

"So why am I even in this discussion? This is my land. He had no right to trade for it with—" Beckett flipped to a page in the contract and jabbed his finger on a line of text. "What's it called, yes — sundries." He leveled his gaze at Dryden's father. "Tell me what the sundries were."

"I don't have to."

Beckett slammed his hand down. "Tell me what the sundries were."

"I have a cousin with a still."

"Yeah. So in exchange for unlimited moonshine my abusive drunk-ass uncle traded my land to you. Nicely played."

He scowled. "I'm not giving up one dime. Not one. Not one bit of land. It's mine. My grandfather gave it to my dad, who also kicked my ass pretty regularly, now that we're being truthful. So I guess I get it because of all that bullshit. All those black eyes, I guess I get my own land. And Dryden I'm not marrying you. Period."

Dryden's lower lip trembled. "But what about my brother? Beckett if anything happens to—"

"I don't see how that has anything to do with me."

Luna placed her hand on Beckett's arm. He exhaled and blinked and turned to her and said softly, "I need a break."

Luna said, "Chickadee I think you and Dilly were planning to serve lunch. Could we have a short recess now while I speak with Beckett for a few minutes?"

"Why yes dear, this is an excellent time for cucumber sandwiches. Will you be willing to stay Ted? We'll get back to this contract right after."

Dryden's father nodded. "We can stay, but I need you to understand Beckett, if you're thinking about fighting us on this, you'll lose. You were underage. Your uncle was allowed to make decisions. Whether you like them or not, I have a signature."

Beckett paused, choosing his words, but Luna gently pulled his arm. "Let's get some air" and led Beckett by the elbow to the front porch.

Roscoe followed a step behind. "Beckett, a word."

Beckett turned with a sigh.

"I know it doesn't seem like it, but this is going to be handled. I can make this go away. I have precedence in a case from Britain in the 1900s."

"Good, I'm trusting you."

"Now I'm going to go in and help Chickie and Dilly wrangle a lunch for these delusional people." He winked and went back in the house leaving Luna and Beckett alone and awkward on the porch.

"Beckett will you come with me to Sunset View?"

He checked his watch. "I probably need to stay close—" But then he glanced at her eyes. They were asking, in the way they did, deep and dark and drawing him in. "Okay, for a few minutes."

Chapter 46

Beckett and Luna stepped onto the small plateau at the top of the mountain. Luna had planted a small garden there, and for the first few months the plants had refused to flower, but now they had burst into a riot of blooms, purples and pinks mostly, the smell of lavender wafting around the old bench that had been there facing west for years.

Luna dropped onto the seat. "Will you join me for a moment?"

"I can't. I—" Beckett was struggling but then he lost, or won, depending on perspective. "Okay."

He sat beside her, stiffly, but then asked, "Can I?" When she nodded, he put both hands up inside her kimono on her stomach. "Baby kicking?"

"A little, right here." She moved his hand to feel the small flutter.

Beckett closed his eyes.

"I'm sorry I barged into the meeting."

Beckett leaned back and sighed. "It's okay, I don't know if I was handling it right asking you not to come. It's all so complicated that—"

"And thank you for telling me about your uncle. I'm so sorry for little Beckie and what he dealt with."

Beckett stared off at the horizon for a few moments. "Well, it's the past. I'm trying to be future-based now."

Luna said, "Yeah."

They both stared at the horizon. Finally she asked, "How do you feel, in your heart?"

"God Luna, I feel crappy. Like there's a weight on my shoulders. I want to be with you, happy, waiting for the baby, just thinking about us and our future, but there's all this crap I have to deal with. And it's like all that past fear is back. My Uncle Jimmy is terrorizing me. Dryden is manipulating me. Her dad is eyeing my land. I just, don't know how to handle it all."

"You love me right?"

He kept his eyes on the horizon. "It's not a big enough word for how I feel about you."

"So turn to me and look at me."

Beckett twisted in his seat.

"You can put your hands on my stomach again if it helps."

Beckett put his hands on the sides of her stomach and closed his eyes.

Luna said, "If this is all you focus on, then it will be easier, I think."

He nodded, his eyes still closed.

"Tell me where you've been the happiest."

Beckett sat for a moment thinking. "I've never been happier than being with you on the deck of the boat. Wait — being with you on the Outpost." He looked up at her. "Anytime in our bedroom. The barn the other day." He grinned sheepishly. "Should I go on?"

"All those times have one thing in common."

"Yeah. You."

"So focus here Beckett. Me, you, our baby. We take up this much space in the world."

"But my land is like an anchor dragging me away."

Luna said, "Yes, I know." She turned to face the horizon again. "And that's why I need to tell you about something."

"Sure, what?" Beckett watched her face.

Luna took a deep breath filling her lungs with lavender and thin mountain air, crisp and warm. The combination causing her head to feel light, like it might pull her away, off up, into the stratosphere. Like a whisper, floating across the miles. "I haven't told you how I came to be alone. And it seems like this might be the right time."

Beckett reached out and took her hand in both of his and kept his eyes down focused there. That was good, because she could only do this if she could fly above him, not being seen. She had to speak this, there was no way to keep it inside anymore, but the speaking of it had to be quiet and still, unnoticed. So yes, Beckett needed to look away. The bee needed to keep buzzing. The flowers needed to waft about their own business. That was the way it had to be. "The night it happened there was a big storm. We knew it was coming. We had been talking about it all day. My dad decided we should paddle for an island. It wasn't too far. We thought we'd have enough time. But on this day we were slow — I think my mom didn't feel good..." Luna gulped and sniffed a deep breath.

"I remember her complaining that she had cramps or..." Her voice trailed off again and a tear welled up in the corner of her eye.

Beckett glanced up at her face, but continued studying the back of her hand, tracing small circles on the soft skin there.

"We paddled. I was bickering with my brother, Xen. He kept telling me I hadn't packed my tent right and I was sick and tired of him complaining about me all the time. So I demanded that mom tell him to stop, but she took his side, said he was right. So while we were paddling, the whole day, I was pissed off. Seething. At everyone." Her voice caught. "That sucked."

The bee spun a lazy circle around the flower and Luna watched it until her breath was back under control. "Then the wind came up. The waves rose and we hadn't made it to the island yet. Dad called it quits and we got in storm-formation and started knotting the boards together."

Beckett pulled her hand to his lips and kissed the knuckle and then replaced it to her lap.

"It was a terrible storm. My dad and brothers were yelling orders at each other. Everything was desperate and tragic and it felt like the end. It lasted for so long, longer than I could bear it. My eyes were closed and I was screaming and then whoosh — a wave grabbed me and shoved me away. I felt the release. Like my knot had just let go."

"Oh god, Luna."

"I opened my eyes and I had my boards but also and—" She chewed her lip, her face screwed up as she tried to gain control over the wave of anguish. "There were about three other boards that were — three empty boards, Beckett." She looked a long way away. "The wind was whipping and I was spinning, and my whole family, some of them were in the water, some out, and then a big wave came and crashed on them while — I saw it all, in the flashes of lightning, and the glow of the sky, but it was so dark too. I know it doesn't make sense, but it was light enough to see it all and too dark to see anything. My dad was in the water and my brother was yelling and my mom was gone and my aunt and my cousin were kneeling and my uncle was clutching the side of — and—"

Beckett gripped her hand so tightly, it hurt, but also kept her present. His knuckles were white with the holding. A cloud crossed the sun, but then puffed away causing the world to go too warm again.

"I tried to paddle to them, but the waves pushed me farther away, and with all the extra boards I couldn't get there. I tried and tried. I didn't want to lose the boards because my family needed them. We wouldn't make it without the boards, but I couldn't paddle with them attached either and so — I kept trying." She shook her head slowly from side to side. "And then in the spot that I was watching, there was nothing, no boards, and no family and I couldn't see anything. So — yeah." Her eyes dropped to the ground. "That's what happened."

"Oh Luna." Beckett put out his arm and she rolled into his chest and sobbed.

He held her, kissed the top of her head, and whispered, "I love you," and "I'm so sorry." Finally, quietly, he asked, "Then what did you do?"

"The storm wouldn't ever stop. I tied myself to my board and waited, churning and rolling and submerging and coming back up for hours until the storm broke. I spent the next three days searching for anyone who might have made it, but I knew they were gone. I paddled to the island, dragging all those boards, and sat there by myself for a long long time. Begging the universe to send them. And after a time I started paddling and found you."

"How long was that?"

"About thirty-four days."

He kissed the top of her forehead and held her tighter. "You've been living with this for a long time."

She clutched his shirt twisting it. "I'll always live with it. I'll never forget it."

He nodded, his cheek rubbing on her hair.

"Beckett, the rope. It was..."

Beckett waited for her words but finally asked gently, "What about the rope?"

Luna clamped her eyes shut. "It wasn't broken or torn or frayed. It was like it had just come undone. I know I knotted it, I'm sure I did. I—" She sobbed more, longer, harder, while Beckett rubbed his hands up and down her shoulder, kissing the top of her head, saying occasionally, shh, and oh god, and I'm so sorry and—

Luna said, "That's why I have to ask..."

She wiped her eyes with the back of her hands, climbed off his chest, and knelt in front of his knees. Before he could even catch on to what was happening, she clutched his hands in his lap.

She pressed her tear stained face to his knuckles. "I have to ask, do we have enough land to buy Dryden's brother's freedom?"

"I don't—what? Damn Luna, it's—"

"Do we have enough to land?" She turned her tear-stained, red-blotched, anguished face up to his.

He nodded slowly.

"Do we have enough land to buy the freedom of those twins? Or the orphan—"

"We do, but—"

"Or the younger brother of your friend from high school?"

"Luna—"

"Or the girl, Cindy, the one who is all alone?"

"Luna you don't understand what you're asking."

"Do we have enough land?"

"It's too much to ask, it's too much—"

"I know it's too much. I understand that, but I'm not asking that, I'm asking if we have enough." Tears rolled down Luna's face.

He searched her eyes and then nodded.

"Because I have to save them. I need to save them, and I need your help. Can you please, please, help me save them?"

"Aw Luna." Beckett curled down over her head, lips pressed into her hair.

"I can't let them die. I have to. Do you understand? I have to."

"You don't even know them."

"I know their names. You know them. Beckett, I can't, please."

They sat quietly huddled while Beckett ran through all that she was asking. "The land is for our baby. To keep our baby safe." He raised up again.

Luna straightened up, wiped the back of her arms across her eyes, and returned to clutching his hands. "Beckett the water is coming. And I heard Chickadee telling Dilly about the fires, and now I can see it, the smoke, over there." She gestured northeast. "And maybe there will be another flu, and the refugees need someplace to go, and we don't have any idea what our baby will need."

"I think the person with the most land wins."

"What if it's the person with the most medicine? Or the largest family? Or the most — I don't know, spit-balling here — boats."

Beckett stroked his fingers down her cheek. "I hear what you're saying but—"

"It's just that you might not survive past tomorrow. I might not survive childbirth. Our baby might not live. We don't know what the future holds, so what is the land for?"

Beckett shook his head. "Nothing, it's just money, in the bank."

"How can we let people die when we know we could save them?"

"I can't, you're right, but also, Luna, someone has to fight the war."

"You did. You fought. Jeffrey fought. He died. And I sat here on the porch waiting, thinking you had died, crying, holding onto Chickadee while she sat in a dark room, afraid, and if I can keep one family from going through that... What are the statistics? If you're young, in the East, what are the chances you'll survive?"

"Seven out of ten."

"Survive?"

"No."

"Beckett, please."

Beckett thought for longer. About how he had been dropped in the East and made to fight with no end game. And how it was being said that the war was all a big ruse to cull the numbers of people, anyway. And how Jeffrey had been culled. And his own great grandfather had been the mayor of this community. And he had grown up with these people and—

"It's like an anchor Beckett. It's dragging you down."

Beckett nodded, his eyes fixed on the horizon, his brow clouded over and stormy.

"Please."

Finally after a long moment, Beckett gripped her hands. "Okay."

Luna looked up. "What?" Her eyes were red and swollen and her cheeks wet.

He put a hand on each side of her face. "We'll pay their taxes."

"All of them?"

"Yes, all of them."

"Will we have anything left?"

"A tiny bit over behind the kitchen gardens back of the house..."

"Do we have enough to keep Jeffrey's sister from having to go now that he's gone?"

"Yes." Beckett nodded slowly, searching her eyes.

"Can we pay the taxes so Sarah can have a baby?"

Beckett hung his head. "Yeah. We can do that."

"Will we have anything left?"

"Our house. The kitchen gardens. I'll need to look at the property lines, if we plot it out maybe we can keep a barn."

Luna paused and pressed her cheek on his fingers. "Do you hate me?" She looked up to read his face when he answered.

Beckett sadly shook his head. "Not at all."

He sat up straighter and ran a hand through his hair. "No, this is going to be all right. I mean, the Monarch Constellation is in the Breeze Constellation after all. We'll get through this. Besides, maybe I didn't need all that land. Most of it was unused, anyway, and what will the government do with it? Log it? Put refugees on it? Grow crops? The government is so overwhelmed that it might sit there doing nothing. So yeah, it's fine. We'll be okay."

Luna climbed up off her knees and sat beside him on the bench. "Would we get to keep this viewpoint?"

"I don't see how, but it would probably take a lot of time and effort to build a fence to keep us out."

He clasped her hand. "It will take some getting used to, that I'm not a big land owner, but also, one less thing to worry about." He gave her a sad smile. "Maybe we should start building boats."

"We're very far away from the coast."

"It's getting closer."

He put a hand on her stomach. He felt for a moment until the baby kicked where his palm was. He leaned down and spoke to the bulge that was their baby. "Your mother is going to save the lives of all these people. That's the kind of person she is. She doesn't even know them. She's a jumper and loves to splash. She has a heart as big as this mountain. And we're not hiding her away anymore. She deserves better than that."

Luna tucked her head on his shoulder. "Thank you Beckett."

"You're welcome."

They looked out over the side of the mountain, the valley dropping below the high noon sun, with a few fluffy clouds overhead.

Luna said, "I want to marry you."

Beckett looked down at her face. "You do?"

"Yes, I was trying to keep our life simple, like we were living on the water. But I love you more than that. You're bigger than that. And our family is growing. I just — if the offer still holds I'd like to."

"Yes, definitely it still holds." He held her hand and then grinned and joked, "But you're sure? I'm not as rich as I was an hour ago."

"It's not the size of your land that I'm attracted to."

He raised his brow and smirked. "That's right, it's the size of my board."

"Yes, indeed."

"All right then, soon to be Mrs. Luna Stanford, we'll tell Chickadee and Dilly and they'll plan it. It can distract them from what I'm about to do."

Luna's stomach growled.

Beckett kissed the top of her head. "Let's go save those lives."

Chapter 47

Beckett began the resumed meeting with a proclamation that shocked them all. "I've changed my mind, Luna and I would like to help the young people on this list pay their service levy. From our land."

Chickadee said, "What are you even talking about Beckie?"

"We should speak about this first, before you do something so rash," said Roscoe sternly.

"I'm sorry Roscoe, I've decided. I mean, we've decided. Luna and I."

"Beckie, all those acres, what are you thinking?" Chickadee wadded up a piece of paper out of frustration.

Beckett chewed his lip. "With Luna's urging, I'm thinking about all those lives."

She leaned back in her chair, her brow furrowed. "Well, that seems purely nonsensical."

"It's not nonsensical. Or maybe it is. Okay, it probably is. But Luna and I lost a friend to this war. We heard about it this morning and we're still reeling from it. And maybe we're acting foolishly…" Beckett gulped and reached back for Luna's hand. "But I don't think so. She's right, I know all these people. And I have enough land to save their lives, so I will. And after I'm done we'll take stock of what we have left and we'll make do."

He took a deep breath and turned to Roscoe. "I'd like you to write up individual contracts with each person on this list. Each family will put forward what they can afford and I'll make up the difference."

Dryden's father said, "We already have a contract."

"It has the signature of my abusive uncle on it. And it ties our families together forever. I won't sign it. I'll fight over it for the rest of my life before I sign it. We're all aware I have the better lawyer. Your guy has been sitting there barely speaking this entire time." Mr Peterson flinched and shuffled papers angrily. Beckett continued, "You'll lose, or you can take my deal, which keeps your son home from war."

"Are you sure about this?" asked Roscoe. "I could win this case, it was just a matter of time."

"Sure, you could. I one hundred percent believe you could. But, also, we decided that we won't watch anybody on that list go fight because they're too poor not to."

Roscoe leaned back in his chair and tapped his pen up and down on the contract. Then he leaned forward and spoke. "What if in the next draft, the stakes are higher, and you have less? How will you pay your own taxes?"

Beckett flinched. And blew out a gust of air. "I can't think about that, what ifs and future problems. I can only do this. So I will."

Roscoe sat back with a long slow breath. "Okay, I'll write it up. Are you in agreement, Ted?"

Dryden's father scowled at Beckett but nodded, shoved his chair away from the table, and ordered Dryden to gather her things.

As they headed to the door Dryden turned back around for one final protest. "You could have told me. Told me that you got your little nomad girl pregnant and that you had to marry her now. You could have saved me the embarrassment."

Chickadee interrupted, "I think you should get used to feeling embarrassed, girlie, it suits you."

Dryden huffed and flounced out of the room.

Beckett pulled Luna's hand up and kissed it.

Roscoe shook his head. "You're sure, absolutely sure about this?"

"No, I'm not. And yes, kind of. It's going against everything I thought I was supposed to do, but Luna hasn't led me wrong so far." He squeezed her hand. "I'm making sure that she and the baby are my biggest priority."

Chickadee said, "I can't understand a word you're saying. You're giving up everything you have."

Beckett said, "Not everything."

"Most everything. Talk some sense into him Dilly. You see what he's doing, make him stop. Be the voice of poetic reason for his sad man-brain."

"I won't." Dilly shook her head. "It's not his brain that's making this decision. It's his heart, and I think his heart might be the wiser."

"Thank you for the vote of confidence, Dilly." Beckett blew out a big gust of air. The one that kept getting stuck in his chest, while he pretended to know what he was doing, saying, thinking. He was relieved to let it go, but also felt deflated that it was gone.

Luna spoke for the first time. "I'm sorry our decision is causing you to feel so upset and worried and I just love you all. I have to do this and I begged Beckett and it's my fault. But please don't be mad at me."

Chickadee said, "Pshaw, child, I'm not mad. Beckett is a grown ass man now, and rich as hell, and I've been living on this land taking care of it, fighting for it, arguing about it, for years, because he was a little boy, and I had to protect him. I could have been producing shows in the city, and well, if most of the land isn't here, I'm going to call myself free to go. But I just want to point out that a year ago this grown ass man bellyached to me that," her voice went up to a falsetto, "'the land was everything to me' and 'his number one priority.' I've heard that so much I can't believe one forty minute conversation could change his mind."

Beckett looked sheepishly at his aunt. "It's for Luna, can you blame me?"

Chickadee sighed melodramatically. "I cannot dear child. She is a beautiful soul. I too would follow her anywhere. Especially after that whole thing earlier about bonking you twice yesterday. Hoo-whee, I thought I would fall right out of my chair!" Chickadee reached over and squeezed Luna's hand. "That there will be a punchline in my next show."

"Now Chickadee it almost sounds like you're saying that you're going to move back to the city," said Roscoe. "As my best-friend, I think you might have to discuss this first. What I would do without you?"

"How can I move back to the city? There's a literal baby about to be born. Are you going to miss it Dilly?"

Dilly said, "That baby will have to get used to me hovering about it every day."

Chickadee said, "Yes, I'm not leaving you dear Roscoe, not this decade, but also, I was talking with Peter, and we have an excellent idea for our next show. So I might travel back and forth for a little while. The film schedule would be a couple of months, and then I'd come back, and see, now I can, because I'm not the caretaker of like a billion acres. I can trust you, Beckie, to be in charge of the one goat you're left with?"

"You can trust me." Beckett had a solemn smirk on his face. "Probably I can keep more than one goat though. It will just be a tighter fit than before."

"So to answer your question, dearest children, no I'm not mad. I actually feel a little liberated. Like a party might be in order."

Luna said, "That's good Chickadee because Beckett and I are going to be married—"

Chickadee jumped from her chair. "Married! Married, do you hear this Dilly?"

It was an unnecessary question, Dilly was already up, rushing them, hugging and tearfully kissing them both.

Roscoe busied himself collecting the papers and smiling to himself. After the hugging was over, Chickadee asked him, "You'll of course get right on the drawing up of paperwork for all of this."

To which he answered, "Of course."

Chapter 48

Two days later at dinner, Dilly clapped her hands and announced, "We need to make wedding plans!" She slammed through a drawer for a notepad and pen. Shark took her excitement as an excuse to jump on her legs.

Then Dilly returned to her chair and held her pen poised above the pad, looking at Luna, waiting.

Luna opened her eyes wide. "Don't look at me, I don't know what the heck this is about!"

"You don't? You haven't been planning your wedding since forever?"

Luna shook her head no.

Chickadee chuckled. "Well, the good news is Dilly has been planning ten different weddings since she was eight, so you can simply nod and smile, dear one, and let her write down whatever she wants."

"What kind of wedding did you have Dilly?"

Chickadee interrupted, "It had all the usual parts, bombastic speeches, mushy vows, drunken relatives, and both brides wore a white dress." She laughed merrily.

Luna squinted her eyes and looked from face to face for the truth.

Dilly asked, "Have you never been to a wedding before?"

Luna shook her head.

Chickadee said, "Well Dilly, you're going to have some fun, aren't you?"

Dilly jotted down a giant number one and circled it three times. "First, we need to discuss a dress."

Luna looked down at her belly. "Do they sell dresses with these dimensions? Couldn't I just wear my normal—"

It was Dilly's turn to look afraid. "Your normal clothes are yoga pants and a floral hand-me-down robe! You wear it open in the front! It won't do for a wedding dress. For one, it's too casual and comfortable."

"So I need an uncomfortable dress?"

Chickadee said, "Exactly! In white, to be impractical too."

Luna said, "Beckett do you hear this? This is complicated, did I not tell you?"

Beckett grinned widely. "You did. You also said I was worth the complications, so here you are, planning the big giant dress you're going to wear. Wait until you see the monkey suit I have to wear."

Luna said, "A suit?"

Chickadee said, "A tuxedo. We'll get his father's cleaned."

Luna said, "Well that might be worth it. I bet you're hot in a suit."

Chickadee said, "Luna those hormones are swinging aren't they child? You're a hot mess one minute and a horny toad the next!" Chickadee giggled some more and scooped up Shark and rubbed her face in the puppy's soft fur.

"I have the best idea!" Dilly clapped her hands, sending her bracelets jingling, "We'll get Chickadee's wedding dress tailored for Luna! Would you like that Chickie, for Luna to wear your—"

"I would love it if she would. There isn't a place in the world it's useful for, and there's plenty of fabric. It would probably make four wedding dresses."

Dilly drew a check mark on her list, mumbling something about Tillie Millerson doing the tailoring. "Okay, flower arrangements, what is your color theme?"

Luna looked at Beckett with wide eyes. "Is this the way it's going to be — for how long?"

Beckett said, "Three weeks."

Dilly said, "Three weeks! How am I going to get all this done in three weeks?"

Beckett grabbed Luna's hand and joked, "Exactly, pick a color, pick a color!"

Luna asked, "Blue?"

Dilly clapped her hands and Chickadee said, "Dear child, hold on to your seat. That's literally the first of a million decisions that mean nothing, but will have to be made as if they're the most important thing in the world. When this is over you'll need a honeymoon."

Beckett kissed Luna's fingertips.

Dilly continued with her list, not listening to anyone around her. "There's your vows of course, you'll have to write them soon."

Luna jokingly collapsed over the back of her chair with an over-dramatic croaking noise. To add to the effect, she crossed her eyes and stuck out her tongue.

Beckett said, "See there Dilly, you killed her. Love of my life, dead, because of your insistence on the wedding of the century."

"This is only going to be the wedding of the decade." Dilly circled the number five on her list and under it wrote: important.

Chickadee said, "Plus, that whole thing, 'love of my life,' you've written your vows already. Say that three times, no one will even notice."

Beckett feigned incredulous. "No one will even notice that I'm reading the same line over and over again?"

Chickadee erupted into laughter. "No one will even notice you at all. They'll be too busy trying to figure out why the bride is wearing your Aunt Chickadee's white tent like a kimono!"

Luna melted into giggles. Beckett and Dilly were laughing.

Chickadee's laughter grew louder and more hysterical. "And why the bride is nine months pregnant but wearing white — trying to pass as a virgin!"

Luna laughed so hard that tears rolled down her face. She snorted loudly. "Oops! I peed myself!" and jumped out of her chair. "Pee running down my leg, darn it!" She bolted out of the room.

Chickadee roared with laughter. "I do love that girl!"

Chapter 49

It was after four a.m. and Luna was up, standing at the porch railing, listening to the dew. She loved this time of day. Misty, usually cooler by degrees, but today it was still hot, or already hot, hard to decide which. There was steam coming off the grass. She shifted her weight and a board creaked. She was usually more cautious with her middle of the night sounds, not wanting to wake anyone. She was the watch after all. The number one rule of the lookout is to let everyone else sleep. Its sole purpose. Especially because land-based people slept soundly and expected it to last, but she was a wanderer, a staring, sometimes worrying, shifting and sighing, watcher of the world.

This morning she was also very uncomfortable. Drips of sweat rolling down her belly to her panties kind of hot. She also felt pretty damn heavy. Also like she needed to burp and fart both. Finally, like she wanted to cry. Happy tears. Mostly.

Footsteps sounded across the living room. She could tell it was Beckett, coming to check.

He peeked his bleary eyed, rumple headed self out of the screen door. "Can't sleep?"

"Not really."

"Me neither," he lied. Beckett always said that, but it was always untrue. He could sleep. As soon as he wanted to, he could. "Mind if I join you?"

"I'd like that."

Beckett dropped into the chair and steadily rocked. "Check out the mist on the gravel. It's beautiful this time of night."

Luna turned and leaned facing him. "Morning, you mean."

"And whatcha thinking about out here?"

Her arms were crossed over her chest against the damp, the dark tendrils of her hair curled on her cheek. Beckett considered brushing one back behind her ear and kissing there.

"You know me, I'm worried about the complex nature of dew vs rain and the velocity ratio between wind and current."

Beckett gave her a smile with a full dimple. "I don't think so, I think you're out here worried about the complexity of the wedding plans."

Luna screwed her face up in pretend-despair. "I am! We talked about wedding dresses and wedding dinners and something called a wedding vow, and now it's hot as hell in here." She leaned over and fanned her belly and her armpit. "It's so hot and I'm like a giant whale and I can't," she pulled her panties out and fanned down into them. "Get cool. How am I going to wear Aunt Chickadee's dress?" She started panting.

Beckett raised a brow, chuckling. "What would help?"

Luna threw her arms out wide. "Water? I want to float. Can we go to Heighton Port? Spend the day with Sarah and Rebecca and Dan?"

"I have another meeting this afternoon with Roscoe, to sign all the individual contracts and pace out the land.

It will be a doozy. I can't — wait—" His face transformed as if a suppressed memory had just been recovered. "I have an idea, there's a lake, small, about two towns over, we could be there in about thirty minutes." He looked down at his bare arm for the timepiece that wasn't there. "We could load up your board and go, right now, eat breakfast there, swim, paddle around, and be back in time for lunch."

Relief washed over Luna. "Could we? That would be awesome. Really—" She kind of felt like crying again.

"Yeah, really. Let's get dressed, quietly."

Thirty minutes later Luna's board jutted from the back of the truck and a basket with some food nestled between them on the seat and Beckett rolled the truck slowly out of the driveway for the mountain road. Traffic was light because of the time of day. The sky still so dark they had to burn the headlights and their windows were rolled down because of the heat. Luna sprawled in the front seat, legs wide, fanning herself. "Is it always so freaking blazing hot?"

Beckett said, "Summer. You've never had the pleasure of a full summer without a place to plunge."

"What's plunging in a lake like?"

"Exactly the same and completely different. No salt, not as floaty."

"Really? Weird."

"Yep and the bottom can be super disgusting. Muddy silt, black, no waves."

"It's like you're describing a foreign world. No waves, what is that?"

"Just follow me."

"Follow you? You're going to swim?"

Beckett grinned over his driving arm. "Of course! I always swim!"

Luna said, "Speaking of swimming, I have to pee."

Beckett scoffed, "You just went, twenty minutes ago."

"Baby has a knee on my bladder."

"I think you're just used to being on the water and going whenever you can put your butt over the edge."

"True that. You Stiffneck land-livers with your toilets." She crossed her legs. "Seriously, if we keep joking and not stopping I might pee in the truck."

He squinted through the front windshield as he pulled the truck into a little store parking lot. There was one other car and through the small window a small light burned inside.

Luna said, "I'll knock and ask them to take pity on me."

"Want me to come—" Beckett's phone rang. "It's Dan."

Luna pantomimed she was going to the store without him, and he nodded while he answered. "Hey! You got the invitation? Yes, it will be good to see you guys. We almost came today, but I have lawyer stuff. Yeah, yeah…"

A few minutes later Luna returned carrying two drinks and three bags of chips. "Junk food! I so needed this." She ripped open a bag, put one foot on the dash near the steering wheel, and one on the passenger door, and propped the bag on top of her stomach with a giggle. "I look like Chickadee."

"Kind of yeah, except she's all soft fluff. You're more stretched out over-expansion about to burst."

The baby kicked and the bag of chips slid down Luna's belly. "Literally burst," she said.

Chapter 50

Twenty minutes later Luna was cautiously stepping down a rocky shore, snaking between pine trees toward a tiny inlet with sky-reflecting water. The sun was coming up. The mud was squelchy, and the water was a little warmer than perfect, but cooler than the air.

Luna pushed the paddleboard out, wading behind it, until she got to waist deep, then she dove under and came up with a splash. "Oh god, that is — oh my god that is amazing."

Beckett had been spellbound watching her, now he returned to himself, tugged his sandals off and dropped his sweatpants, revealing some swim trunks.

Luna cocked her head to the side.

Beckett waded in two steps but stopped mid-step. One foot was up, one arm bent awkwardly. "What?"

"This is new for me, and super sexy."

He waded a couple more steps, grimacing, jerking and uncoordinated. "You, madam, are too horny."

It was true what he said. She was totally hormonal, but also, his muscles, and tattoos, and he was in the water, and oh! He dove in, swam under, and his hands grasped her ankles, tugging her under. He rose, his head popping up in front of her face, making her feel breathless and wiggly. She wrapped her arms around his wet head, nose to nose, treading water.

His arm was on the paddleboard, his other hand on her hip, holding, wriggles and flutter kicks.

A drip of wet down his nose, her cheek against his, wet breaths in between. "It's like the day you jumped off the boat, you found me, in the whole ocean, you found me."

"And I'll keep finding you. Over and over."

He adjusted his arm over the board and pulled her thigh up around his waist, wet slippery skin on skin.

She kissed him. She pressed up against him. Their legs gracefully kicking and wrapping, Their hands rubbing. Finally she pulled her panties off and with a splash flopped them onto the board. He chuckled and pulled his shorts off and splashed them onto the board. "Don't lose them, we'll be naked to the world."

Luna wrapped her legs around his waist, Beckett ran his hands down her to her hips and pulled her close and they made love, splashing and twisting and holding on and floating and whispering sweetnesses into each other's ears, just the two of them, in the water, in a deserted part of the world, on the edge of a mountain, at sunrise.

Until done, Beckett yelled to the sky, "I love you Luna Stanford!"

"I love you too, Beckett Stanford."

Still treading water, she pulled her panties on and he pulled up his shorts. "So how do you ride this thing?"

Luna opened her eyes wide. "Seriously? You have never been hotter than this morning. Is it because you're aware I'm writing something called wedding vows?"

"Yep, you need to be well-sexed so you'll be extra romantic in front of all the guests."

"Wait, how many guests?"

"Not that many, and now I'm changing the subject again. How do I ride this?" He smiled with a full-dimpled smile.

"You climb up. Then you crouch in one movement, but pause, catch your balance, and then stand. All you have to do after that is keep your eyes on the horizon and paddle."

Beckett splashed his top half onto the board and rocking and rolling got his whole body on top of it. He flipped over with a splash and a groan. "Don't worry I've got this." He mounted it again and rose to a flailing crouch. His arms waved around and he rocked maniacally.

Luna was treading water with languid loops of her arms and small leg flutters. "You are so hot, eyes on the horizon, now stand."

He wobbled up to a full stand.

"You forgot the paddle." Luna swam forward, grabbed the paddle off the board, dove up, and placed it into his outstretched hand. "Now paddle."

Very slowly, with jerks and spasms, he lowered the paddle into the water, pushed it back, and propelled the board forward.

Luna said, "That is the most beautiful thing I've ever seen."

He called back over his shoulder, "You need to get out more."

"Now turn back."

"How? Oh crap, I'm heading out to sea, I'll be lost, crap!"

"Beckett, you're on a lake, and you're only fifteen feet away. I'll swim to you before you get to twenty-five feet, promise."

"Okay then, but what do I do?" He wobbled reck-lessly but corrected himself. "I'm going farther — what do I do?"

"Push the paddle in and back and it will spin you, like that, perfect. Now paddle on the other side, twice. Okay, see? You're coming around."

Beckett turned. "Thank you. I can see you again."

"Now paddle toward me. Don't look down. Look at me, over here. Or the horizon actually." Beckett pulled the board up close. "How did I do?" His board tipped, and he careened, arms spinning, and fell with a giant splash. He came up with a grin.

"You did great."

"Better than Dan?"

"Much better than Dan. Want me to take you for a spin?"

Beckett climbed on the board and kneeled with Luna standing behind him. She paddled them around some of the coast line, exploring inlets and small marshy places, until finally her stomach started growling. "I'm famished."

"Me too, let's go see what we have left to eat."

They hauled the board out of the water and slid it into the bed of the truck. In the front seat they popped open another bag of chips and ate them talking about the lovely morning and the beautiful lake and the weather. Luna said, "It's one of the first times I've ever spent this much time on land with no one else around."

Beckett blinked a few times. "Yeah, it's weird. I won-der why?"

Luna took another big bite of chips. "Also no traffic, like no one is interested in coming here, but it's so pretty."

Beckett grew pensive. "Yeah. Yeah. Right. You know, maybe we ought to go."

He backed the truck up the small incline and pulled out onto the road. There wasn't any traffic. At all. It hadn't been a big deal at five a.m., but now, at ten a.m., it was notable. And causing Beckett's mind to whir. What was happening -- what had he missed?

Luna noticed his mood changing. "It's probably no big deal, maybe they have security now, like you plan to have on your mountain."

Beckett looked over at Luna. She looked nervous because he was nervous. He had no real reason to be nervous, just a feeling, and those were usually stupid and unnecessarily punishing to his brain. He clapped a hand on her thigh. "How about this morning, huh? That was fun, right?"

"We should do it all the time, whenever we can."

"Definitely. We will."

Chapter 51

They drove for a bit longer. "Here's the store I stopped at earlier. We should get some more snacks, take them home to Chickadee. She'll adore us for it."

Luna said, "Do you think she can adore you any more than she already does?"

"I doubt it, but we shall see." He pulled the truck into a spot directly under an old sign that read: General Foods and Gas. The lot was still empty except for the same car from five hours ago. Luna jumped out. "Gotta go to the bathroom again! At least I know where it is."

Beckett got out slower. He scanned the parking lot and the woods beyond before he walked across the pavement to the door and opened it. There was a bell that announced his entrance, but no sounds within. Beckett called, "Hello?"

At the coolers he grabbed a cola for Luna and a root beer for himself, then another lemon lime soda for Luna for later. He stacked them in his arms and headed for the chips and candy bars, glancing around again for any sign of life.

Then the back door opened and with a deep scary frightening rattling cough, someone walked into the shop. Beckett watched from behind the shelving. It was a woman, wrapped in a sweater, haggard and definitely sick.

She wheezed for breath, then whooped, gasped, and wheezed again. Her chest rattled with phlegm. Coughs echoed through the tiny shop. Possibly following the flinging spittle, flying around the air, adhering to things. To people. To Beckett. She coughed again.

Beckett said, "Oh um, I was just—"

The cough started again, thick and bone-chilling.

Beckett walked toward the counter. He did not want to get closer, but he needed to see the person, check her for the telltale sign.

She huddled over the counter holding a rag to her mouth, a rag tinged-pink, sopping.

Beckett looked through the window over her shoulder and saw Luna, smiling, trailing across the parking lot from the bathroom to the truck. She looked fresh, healthy, glowing.

The woman rasped, "Surprised the quarantine didn't keep you away, but probably you were already exposed, right?"

The color drained from Beckett's face.

She coughed, rattled, hacked, and spit into the rag. "Back fifteen years ago, wasn't it, the Deep Flu? Well, it's back with a vengeance." She put both hands on the counter and gasped for breath. "Taking all of us it didn't get last time."

The bags and drinks spilled from Beckett's arms to the counter.

"Yep, surprised you're here." She wheezed and struggled for air.

"Never mind on the stuff, yeah, um..." Beckett backed to the door.

"I would have thought the quarantine would keep everyone away, but this morning I had a pregnant girl in here." She raised her chin and exposed her neck, dark, purple. The way Beckett's mother's neck had looked just before — "I didn't want to scare her, but this place is a death sentence—"

Beckett slammed his back into the door, pushed out, and spun into the parking lot. He had lost all feeling in his hands — shaking — the blood rushing all over inside him except where it needed to go, his extremities. He yanked his keys from his pocket and his mutinously shaking appendages dropped them in the dirt. His breath was gasping, crap — he was going to panic. Nope, he was full panicked. This was — he bent for his keys and tried to catch — he was going to pass — he glanced up.

Luna was in the passenger seat watching him through the truck's back window. He tried to get the keys into his right hand, but his fingers wouldn't listen to his brain. He tried to pull the door open, but also slammed against it, and then yank pulled, but couldn't — he had to get Luna out of here, now, right now—

Luna opened his door from the inside. "Beckett, what's wrong?"

"Can't — breathe—"

She grasped his wrists and pulled him into the seat.

He collapsed down and wriggled his hands from her grasp. "Don't touch me. God it's everywhere—" He grasped at his collar and tugged, trying to get air into his lungs.

"Beckett what happened? Beckett, put your head back." She pushed him back in the seat and rubbed his chest and shoulders, made to climb on his lap. "What's happening?"

"No, don't — she was sick. Luna, don't touch me, I'm—"

Luna sat on his lap and rubbed her hands down his cheeks.

"Don't Luna you'll get — God I can't breathe."

"Shhhhhh, Beckett, shhhhhh." She put her forehead on the headrest beside his ear. "Tell me."

"She was sick. Was she in there — when you went there? The bathroom. Luna, oh god, the bathroom. You bought chips, you ate — if something happens to you, the baby. I have to get you out of here." He brought the keys to the ignition but his shaking hands couldn't aim. He dropped his hand with the key to the seat beside him. "I can't do anything right, I brought you to a fucking quarantined town."

"Shhhh, Beckett, shhhhh. Try to breathe, please, breathe."

"Do you know if you've been exposed to it? The Deep Flu, have you had it?"

"I don't know."

"It was fifteen years ago, you can't remember?"

"I was four. I don't remember being sick."

"How about your family, did you lose anyone, fifteen years ago, maybe they would have talked about losing relatives to it?"

Luna said, "I'm sorry Beckett, I just don't know."

Beckett sat for a moment staring around wildly, anywhere but her eyes. He needed to wash. She needed to wash. He had to get her home. Luna was on his lap, her rounded belly pressed into his stomach, her body folded on his chest, her head beside his ear. He couldn't touch her but she was everywhere all around.

He began to recite what he knew. "It's called the Deep Flu. Fifteen years ago it killed seven out of ten people. My parents. Those that had it and survived are considered immune, like me. But if you haven't had it, or if it's mutated, or — the incubation is six days. After that it can kill in a day."

Luna said into his ear, "Oh."

"Without knowing if you've ever had it, we'll have to put you in quarantine, and just—"

Luna pulled a hair's breadth away to look at the side of his face.

"I don't know what I'll do if something happens to you."

Luna closed her eyes tight and nestled into the side of his neck and spoke just above his heartbeat. "This can't be how it ends. Just breathe okay?"

"Yeah, of course, yes. I need to drive now, sitting in this parking lot is freaking me out."

Luna climbed off his lap to the passenger seat and Beckett reversed the truck from the space and onto the empty road.

Part Three:

Home

Chapter 52

Beckett banged into the house. "Chickadee! Dilly!"

Chickadee bustled in from the kitchen. "What, dear boy?"

He stood in the middle of the living room, hands on his head. "I took Luna to Highland Glen, to the lake."

Dilly froze in the doorway.

"I didn't know it was under quarantine. She's been exposed—"

Chickadee interrupted, "Now why would you go there? Aren't you listening to the news?"

"No, I'm not, and this isn't helping. Dilly, help?"

Dilly recovered herself. "Yes, yes, of course." She rushed forward and grabbed Luna around the shoulders. "First thing we should—"

Beckett said, "She needs to shower. I need to shower. You just touched her, so you should probably shower too."

Dilly asked, "How exposed do you think you were?"

Beckett said, "Luna used a bathroom. Twice. I stood not two feet away from someone with a blood cough."

Chickadee said, "Out to the porch with you both, strip down, oh dear, dear, and we'll burn the clothes."

Luna was terrified.

She couldn't tell if she was more scared of the what ifs of the sickness or that Beckett and Dilly and Chickadee were so freaked out that they were thoughtlessly ordering each other around and no one was talking directly to her or explaining anything to her or —

Chickadee said, "Dilly you'll need to gather your tinctures and remedies. I'll call Roscoe and tell him we're not going to make the appoint—"

Dilly asked, "Should we go to the hospital?"

Chickadee waved her away. "We can't, the hospital is full of people dying from this flu. If Luna wasn't exposed, she would be — and the baby." She glanced around at everyone. "Is no one watching the news?"

Beckett said, "All we watch around here are comedies. So forgive me for not paying attention to the state of the world."

"Comedies are for escape, but you still have to know!"

They all stopped short, noticing Luna, a woeful expression, a tremble on her bottom lip.

Beckett said, "I'm sorry, love. I know this is overwhelming. You just need to take a shower now, okay?"

Luna nodded, a tear rolling down her cheek.

He strode to the front porch and stripped from his clothes, pulling his shirt over his head, dropping his shorts to the floor, kicking out of his sandals last, because he couldn't think straight. Luna stripped off her clothes too, kicking them into the same pile. Then she followed Beckett naked through the house to the steaming shower.

Chickadee called from the kitchen, "Dilly and I will bring in towels for you."

The shower was not luxurious, or relaxing, or sexy, it was busy. They wordlessly soaped and scrubbed every bit of their bodies. Beckett covered his hair with soapy suds and scrubbed around and around. He poured out a dollop of shampoo and lathered it into Luna's hair and scrubbed vigorously, and then they rinsed each other of all the soap. And even with the proximity, their naked bodies, it wasn't enough to distract them from the mood — desperate, sad, terrified.

A few minutes later they emerged from the shower to fresh towels, a couple of t-shirts, and clean underwear. Beckett's pale skin was pink from the heat and scrubbing, Luna's darker skin glowed, her black hair glistened.

Steam drifted around the bathroom as they dressed, sticky and thoughtful. Luna caught a glimpse of Beckett shaking his head as he pulled his underwear on. "What?"

He leaned on the sink. "I can't believe I did that. I'm so sorry Luna, please be okay, I'm so sorry that I did that."

She threw her arms around him and he clutched her to his chest, kissing her hair. "I'm sorry."

After a moment she pulled away and wiped her eyes. "I should go out and see what Dilly wants me to do next."

———————————

Beckett and Luna were seated at the table, side by side, plates of dinner in front of them, heads drooping, barely able to eat. Tea steeped in mugs drifting steamy fragrance around the room. The combination of fear and too much garlic in the food and wafting peppermint caused Luna's head to spin. They all ate in silence.

After Luna pushed her plate away, full enough, Dilly pulled a box from the top shelf of a cabinet. "I have tinctures and remedies next." She dug out wooden box holding an assortment of small vials. "A few oils."

She twisted a lid. "A couple of drops in your tea."

Luna said, "Just as long as it's safe for the baby."

Dilly stopped in mid-drop, holding the vial over the tea mug, her hand shaking. "I don't know. Oh god, I don't know." She looked around at their faces, then burst into tears, and began digging through the box. "I don't know if they are. I don't know. What am I going to do?"

Chickadee jumped up and held her. "Dilly dear, take a deep breath, this is — you know this. You sat at enough bedsides to know how to do this." Dilly stared down into the box. "But Luna — the *baby*."

Luna was watching, tears sliding down her face.

Chickadee said, "Just one drop and then another. What's the first thing?"

"These minty oils."

"Sure, of course, they're probably fine, right, Luna?"

Luna said, "That sounds okay. Maybe nothing directly on my stomach."

Chickadee nodded her head looking from Luna back to Dilly. "Exactly, and we'll read the ingredients. Right Beckett, right Luna?"

Beckett nodded. He was having trouble watching, he was instead focused on a fork.

Dilly decided on three small bottles. "Okay, these are — I'm so sorry Luna." She sniffled. "I didn't mean to scare you. This was simply a small little freak out, but I'm better now. I only need to mix a couple of things. Please don't let my little breakdown worry you."

"It's okay Dilly, we're all scared. give me the first thing."

Dilly squirted three drops into Luna's tea and gave Beckett oils to massage onto Luna's feet.

Chickadee dropped into a chair and watched, chewing her lips, quieter than Luna had ever seen her.

Beckett held Luna's feet in his lap and rubbed them silently.

Dilly puttered around, reading from a book of recipes, mixing, chopping, passing things to Luna to take.

Finally Dilly said, "That's all we can do, for now. I'll give you more tomorrow." She put the box away on a lower shelf.

They all four sat for a minute. Then Chickadee banged her hand down on the table. "Well, I for one think we need find some way to uplift this pissy-ass mood. My shows are on, and we could all use a laugh. I'll pop popcorn. "

Dilly said, "I don't know, popcorn might not be. . ."

"I insist. Would you like popcorn Luna?"

"I Would. With butter."

"No harm in butter. Butter is literally the only good thing in the world."

Chickadee popped the corn while Dilly warmed the butter.

Beckett found his ability to speak again. "You okay with this?"

Luna nodded. "I could definitely use the laugh."

Chapter 53

Chickadee sank into her reclining chair, with a bowl of popcorn perched on her stomach. Dilly perched at one end of the couch, with another bowl in front of her. Luna sat at the other with pillows all around her legs and belly for support. Beckett chose to sit on the floor, leaned back in front of Luna. She wrapped her fingers in his growing hair and he wrapped and arm around her calf. Shark sat beside Luna curled up asleep.

The shows came on, they were funny, hilarious at parts. Luna allowed herself to switch into a better mood. She giggled and her laughter was infectious. Dilly turned the lights down and the glow from the television lighting their faces, giving them a focal point, helped them ignore the stark reality of what they might be waiting for — six days. But in the in-betweens, the pauses between jokes, the moments before the ad jingles came on, the distraction gone, it would come back — six days.

During an ad for protein bars Luna thought, *six days* of tinctures and remedies and worried faces and *maybe I'm going to die. Maybe the baby will die.*

The baby kicked.

Luna put her hand on her stomach feeling the baby's familiar toss and turn, fluttering under her ribcage, rolling across her whole stomach.

The show returned from the commercial break, the family in this story, sat around a table exchanging wise-cracks. The son was being a total ass, but his mom deserved it, she was really, really stupid.

And Beckett was watching intently. The glow of the images flickered across his impassive face.

Luna reached for Beckett's hand and pulled it to her stomach, and in an instant his attention shifted, from show to baby. He placed a hand on each side of her stomach and kissed the front of it as Luna curled down and kissed the top of his head.

Dilly said, "Aw, you guys are the best. Do you see this Chickadee?"

"I do, I see it. They're making me all weepy-eyed right when I'm trying to enjoy this comedy." She pushed a handful of popcorn in her mouth.

Beckett kissed Luna's stomach again. "Want to go to bed now?"

Luna nodded. He stood and led her by the hand to their room.

Luna climbed into the sheets on her side, and pushed a pillow between her knees to support her upper leg, this pregnancy thing had gotten very uncomfortable. Beckett pulled his shirt over his head and climbed in behind her and wrapped around her body. His hand on the side of her stomach. His mouth on the back of her head.

"Is this what we have to do now, for six days?"

"Just lay in bed and wait."

"Oh."

He kissed the back of her hair, a long kiss, that stayed, and—

Her shoulders began to shake. He pulled enough away to ask, "Luna?"

She continued to cry, tears wetting her cheeks and rolling down to her pillow.

He tried to pull her face up to explain, but she curled it tighter down into her fists and cried harder. He understood, if anyone deserved a cry it was Luna on the day she found out their road trip might have been her death sentence. But her lonely tears made him panic. He wanted to grab her into his arms and rush her out, to somewhere, safe. Secure. Alive.

Where would that even be? Not the hospital. Luna wasn't even going there for the birth. She had decided to stay home, find a midwife. Beckett had agreed because in his experience people checked into the hospital sick and never came home. Like his parents. Like so many people at his school. Like most of the people on the mountain.

"Luna please say it."

She sobbed. "I hate it here."

His body tensed, the familiar constriction around his chest, lungs squeezed. "Me?"

She cried harder, unable to speak, ashamed of the words.

"I'm so sorry. I just wanted to make you happy. I swear I wanted to keep you safe and I—"

She sobbed more, tears wracking her body.

Beckett held on as if she were the last board in a violent storm. He thought she was going to pull away, that their knot would go, and that would be it — but if he could just hold on.

Like choking she said, "It's being on land. It's so mean. And scary. I don't understand this world. Why it's like this. How it can be so awful."

Beckett turned her to her back, kissed her shoulder, and nestled into her neck. "I know baby, I know. It is. I'm sorry it is. If I could protect you from it, I would."

"But you can't. You try, and it's. . ."

She looked up at the ceiling. "I miss the ocean. It was simple there. I only had to worry about the weather."

Beckett stilled. The knot was loosening. She was pulling away. "But the weather Luna. That was big too."

She blinked on the tears welling in her eyes, still staring at the sky. "I understood it. I navigated by the stars. I can't even see the stars in here. I miss the currents and splashes and glistens and waves. I love you. I love Chickadee and Dilly, you're my family and I can't imagine life without you, but I miss not being scared. I'm so scared."

Beckett dropped his head to the pillow. "You're scared all the time now?"

Luna nodded.

"I haven't been home for very long, I feel like, if given the chance, I could fix this, make it better. We have to wait for six days but the—I screwed up Luna, I took you to the lake without researching first. Can you please give me more time to make this work? I'll do better, I'll make our home happier. I promise."

Luna looked up into his eyes. "Oh Beckett. I'm not leaving you. This isn't me saying that I'm leaving you. This is me saying that I have to go back to the ocean, once the baby is here and ready, and that, please, please come with me because I can't live without you."

Beckett searched her face and then nestled his face into the soft part between her neck and shoulder. "I can't live without you either. Please make it through."

"I'm trying."

"Me too. Just please. Hold on. Okay? Live through. If you can. I'll fix this. I'll make it better."

204

Luna stroked her hand down his cheek. "I know, you'll try. You will. We'll lay here and try to keep me alive, and we'll get married and have a baby, and we'll try to make this work." She gave him a sad smile.

Beckett said, "That's not exactly what I mean, I mean yes to all that, but also I'll build a boat."

"Oh." Luna pulled away and drew her eyebrows together. "You'll build a boat for me?"

"I will."

"I'm lying here in a puddle of tears, telling you that I hate this place and you're saying," she lowered her voice, "I'll build you a boat?"

"I'll have to figure out how, but yes."

"You aren't mad? I mean I love it too. It's home, but I miss the ocean so much."

Beckett kissed her on the top of her head and thought for a few minutes. "I know that, and it's okay. We'll live here when we need to, but we'll have a boat."

"You're surprising me. I thought you hated the ocean."

"Well, a beautiful and wise young lady once told me that I had a lot in common with my great-great-great-grandfather, a sea captain, and ever since I've been re-evaluating my stance on the sea. I figure, what the hell, let's build a boat."

"Beckett I adore you." Her smile turned happy. "Do you even know how to build a boat?"

"I have tools." He smiled his full dimpled smile. "That same beautiful woman said I look really hot when I'm wearing my tool belt. So yeah, I'm sure past that it's just easy."

Luna giggled. "Easy to build a boat?"

"The girl I'm in love with has mad skills too, she can probably figure it out."

"She sounds awesome."

Beckett tightened his arms around her shoulders. "She is, and this is what I'm saying, what I've been saying. Me and you, we, we're doing this right? Right now we're land-based, but when we need to, we'll float. You saw me on the paddleboard this morning. I'm one more day away from living on one."

Luna solemnly shook her head. "That's not exactly what I saw."

"You haven't considered this: Have I ever not done what I set out to do?"

Luna blinked and did indeed consider. "No, you always do it."

"So see. Boat is as good as built. Maybe I have to buy one, I might have more money than actually ability, but the intent is the same. I love you, Luna."

"I love you too."

"Get some sleep, you'll need rest to kick this."

Luna kissed him under the jawline and tucked into his chest to sleep.

Chapter 54

On the third day of Luna's quarantine, Dilly was out in the back field and Chickadee had taken a call and stepped out onto the porch leaving Beckett and Luna finishing their breakfast. Beckett cleared away their dishes and pulled down the box of remedies and took out a small notebook and the thermometer. "So, we need to take your morning temperature again, so we can have a base reading for the—"

"Why?"

Beckett turned to her with the thermometer in his hand. "You know why, so we have a base reading, your normal temperatures, so on day six —"

"Yes, so we can see if I have a temperature spike on day six. So we can know-know, but why, if it's not helping? It's just worrying—"

"It's not helping, it's not just anything, but—" Beckett gripped the thermometer. "I don't know what to do, Luna. I don't have the skill set for saving your life. Not from this. I can build a wall. I can toss sandbags. And I can shoot. I have enough guns, tucked away in this place, if people wanted to hurt you, I could stop them. If they made it up the mountain, past my neighbors to Mountainview Pass? I could sit on the roof over the porch and pick them off before they got within sight of the house. I wouldn't even be scared because I can do it. Kill them before they get to you. I learned it in the Army and I was good at it. It sucks that that's what I know. I should have gone into the Navy, Dan was a hundred percent right about that. But I don't know how to save you from this sickness. I don't know at all. So Dilly showed me how to use this thermometer, and she told me to write your temperature down in the morning, at noon, and after dinner, so we would know. And it's all I've got. Maybe it's the dumbest thing in the world to do, but it's all I've got."

Luna moved around the table, stood quietly in front of Beckett, and pushed her hair back from her forehead. His hands shook as he pressed the thermometer to her temple and counted to five. Then he glanced at it's screen and transcribed the number, 99.1, under last night's temperature, 98.9. He didn't know if that tiny uptick was a statistical anomaly or a terrifying portend, but either way it was noted.

Luna waited for him to finish and then asked him to go for a walk. "Show me something you haven't shown me yet." After a long day full of whispers and, "How are you feeling?" And "take this too, swallow it down," and "you should sit down and rest dear." She wanted to go long and far away.

Beckett led her along a path, through the woods, in a direction she hadn't gone before. She had always walked west toward the viewpoint, or east to the sunrise field, but today Beckett took her to the south. The path joined a dirt road for a quarter mile, and then separated from it, crossed a field, and dove back through the woods, for so long that Luna had to ask, "All of this is yours?"

"Yes, and more."

"Oh."

He helped her clamber over a fallen tree. Until the path turned out of the tree line at a craggy cliff. Beckett swept out an arm. "Bug Boulder."

A boulder as big as a shed stood to the side of the path, warming in the direct sun. Luna said, "Tell me about it."

"This is where I used to hide after my mom died. When my dad was pissed. When Uncle Jimmy was out of his mind."

Luna put her hand out and pressed it to the side of the warm rock. "Little Beckie would come all this way by himself?"

"I slept here too. Sometimes for days."

Luna took in the scope of it. "You'd sleep on top of this rock, no shelter?"

Beckett grinned. "See, that's where you're wrong. That's why this is such an excellent hiding place. Yes, you can sit and sleep on top. And pretend like you're riding a bug I might add. That was cool." He picked his way around the smaller rocks at the front of the Boulder. "But over here. . ."

Luna followed him around the rock.

"See how the cliff curves over right here? The Boulder juts out right here, like a cave."

Luna cocked her head. "It's really small, you could fit in there?"

"It was tight, but it worked for its purpose. It kept me mostly dry."

Luna turned around. "You would be out here in the rain?"

"It rains a lot."

"True, and I was out in the rain a lot growing up, but land-based animals don't usually choose to sleep outside."

"There wasn't a lot of choice in the matter."

"Yeah, poor little Beckie." She rubbed her fingers down his arm, feeling the taut muscles under his skin. He clenched when he couldn't relax. "We have a lot in common, you and I, you floating here, under a big sky. Except you were alone. I had my whole family with me. You're crazy brave to sleep here."

Beckett's mouth turned up in a half smile. "I felt like a coward at the time."

"Little kids don't understand much about the world do they?"

"Not at all." He picked a path to the back of the boulder, where it met the cliff, and with two leaping steps deftly climbed to the top. "Come up?"

She laughed. "You made that look easy!"

"Ah now see, the tables are turned, just pop up here."

Luna picked a place for her hand and with some awkward scrambling, and Beckett pulling her up by the other hand, she made it to the top. She joked, "I totally would have made it by myself if it wasn't for the baby."

Beckett chuckled. "I have no doubt."

Luna appraised the spot. "You're up high, but there's not much view. Too many trees over there."

"They cut down on the wind and keep the temperature a little better, but a view would have probably terrified me, Bug Boulder is for staring up at the sky." Beckett dropped down to a sitting position and lounged back. "Except when I was nine I fit, now I'm way long, my legs hang off."

Luna looked down at him for a moment, then dropped down beside him, looking up at the sky. "Oof, lying on my back is too uncomfortable." She curled to her side.

Her eyes traveled across his lips to the indent of his dimple to his angled jaw and down the taut neck muscle that stretched to the collar of his shirt, disappearing at that small spot she loved to kiss, right at the base of his throat, where his mind and heart met and gave them voice. It vibrated, with heartbeat and current and possibility, and she would keep her lips there forever if she could.

He asked, "What are you thinking about?"

"You." She trailed a finger along the edge of his neck.

He lifted her fingers to his lips, kissed them, and placed them over his heart. The sun was warm on their skin. The stone warm on their backs.

"Beckett I need you to promise me something."

"Anything."

"If something happens to me—"

"God Luna, not that, don't."

"Beckett. If something happens to me. . ."

He shook his head.

"If something happens. . ."

"Please don't."

"Just listen, my love, okay? If something happens to me, if I'm not here, don't do this. What you do when you hide from the world — alone. Don't live here at Bug Boulder. Don't run away to an Outpost. Don't be alone."

"I can't hear this, please stop."

"You have to hear it, and you have to promise me. If I'm not here, don't be alone. Surround yourself with people. I want you to live with Sarah and Dan, he loves you so much. You live with them, with Rebecca, with your aunts, you build as many rooms as you can on this house, or one giant boat, and you live with all of everyone. Promise me."

"I don't want to think about it."

"I know you don't, but if you don't promise me, I'll call Roscoe and make him write it down in something called a will, and you'll have to listen to Roscoe tell you to do it."

"That would be worse."

Luna nodded solemnly. "I also want you to go look for Sky and her family and make sure they're okay. When you find them I want you to ask them what they need and whatever they want, you give it to them. You can find them because you can do anything."

"Is that all?"

"Yes, promise me you won't be alone."

"Okay, Luna, I promise."

"Good. Thank you."

Beckett turned his face back toward the sky. "Shit man, that sucks."

"Yeah." She tucked her head up onto his chest and he wrapped an arm around her shoulders. She reached over and draped her hand over his bicep feeling the strength just under his skin. She traced her fingers down and along his tattoo of the trees. "Now I see, those trees, they're from here."

"Yes."

"When you remember this place, those trees, when you look down at your tattoo, does it give you happy memories or sad?"

"Awful memories."

"So why did you get the tattoo?"

"To remind myself I guess, I'm nostalgic about this place, even though it doesn't deserve it. Nothing good ever really happened here except escape."

"Escape is pretty good. Surviving is a good thing."

"Surviving kind of sucks if you're left behind."

Luna trailed a hand down his chest to his stomach and ran a finger along and under the edge of his pants back and forth. She wiggled up and met his lips and they kissed. Deep and long until his pants stretched against his want of her. She whispered into his ear. "Want to play a game?"

"What's it called?'

"Don't rock the boat." She traced her fingers down the front of his pants and pressed against him.

He caught his breath. "How do you play?"

"You both climb onto one paddleboard."

"Done."

She jumped up over him. "You should have on less clothes, no self respecting Waterfolk man would invite someone to play Don't Rock the Boat without having his pants off already."

Beckett stripped off his shirt. "Man, there are a lot of rules for you people." He undid the button on his shorts and wiggled them off and down and kicked them over the side.

"Now lay back." She slowly, teasingly, stripped off her clothes piece by piece and sat astride his lap. She leaned to his ear. "How bad do you want me?"

"So bad."

"Good, because you need to really, really, really want me." She hovered above him, a centimeter of distance between her body and his.

His hands rubbed up her thighs. "Done."

"Now here's the game — you can't touch me."

"Oh." He pulled his hands away.

She sat down on him with a small gasp. Her breath quickened. "Now neither of us can move. We have to be completely still. No water can lap over the side of the board, or we lose." She pressed her forehead to the edge of his cheek. "And we can't touch or move or speak."

She could hear his breath fast in her ear. The need to move against him was building, He felt electric, pulsing,

She trembled and her breaths pulled in, drawing him closer and pushing him down.

Barely audibly he said, "God."

Her blood coursed. Keeping on top of her racing heart took physical effort. The top of her lip tasted of salt.

His arms drew up off the rock and hovered, still, just above the skin of her legs. She felt him tightening, every inch drawing closer, deeper, further in. Her body was magnetic, or his, she pulled down, weighting, liquid rolled down her skin, eddied in her flats, filling her voids. She breathed out, "How bad?"

He moaned, "God," again.

"Don't talk, we don't want to lose."

"Can't—"

She moved her mouth a little closer to the steady thrum of his neck hovering, she could lick there if there weren't rules. He tightened below her, pushing slightly.

She whispered, "Shhhhhhhh," and then, "look at the sky."

Her eyes focused on the curve of his jaw, the shadow and shelter of its curve. For a long trembling few minutes they paused, still, but their insides quivered and vibrated.

Beckett's breath drew in. He whispered, "Fuck, don't move, Luna, butterfly, on your shoulder, it's right there. An inch from my face."

"Really? The tickle?"

His body went completely still. Luna concentrated on the tickle on her left shoulder, until after a moment it was gone.

Beckett's breath escaped him and then he grabbed her roughly by her hips and pulled her body up and down desperately, fast and slamming. Luna pushed hard against his chest, pulling on his skin, a moan erupting with the vibration that built and pushed from their bodies, with their breath and with a wave, and it was over.

"Fuck that was amazing."

Luna licked up the side of his neck, allowing herself the taste she had been longing for. "I think we tipped the boat."

"Nah, we won that game, that was — a fucking butterfly Luna, on your shoulder."

"What color was it?"

"Dark blue and black, wow, that was, oh my god."

She curled her head down on his chest, and his arms went up and around her. They huddled there for some long moments. "Don't get dressed yet. Can we just be naked here on Bug Boulder?"

"Definitely." She sat up on his lap and looked down at her stomach. His hands drew to it and rubbed and caressed it's round firmness. The baby kicked his palm and rolled from one side of her belly to the other. She watched Beckett's eyes. She loved how they would go wide whenever the baby kicked and then he would sigh and relax into the moment. She asked, "How do you feel about this place now?"

He looked up at her, sky above her face, above him, the weight of her on his hips, the baby nestled, growing in her stomach, his heart heavy, but the taste of her salt on his lips, and his breath skipping because of the butterfly wing that had pulsed beside her heartbeat at her throat. "It joined my list of happy places."

Chapter 55

Luna walked every day, sometimes with Beckett some times without. If she was alone, she checked in occasionally by phone, because everyone was worried now all the time. There was a feeling of: Maybe This Is It, My Last Moment with Luna.

And she couldn't blame them. She felt as if everything might be her last time. She got misty-eyed holding Beckett's hand. They couldn't have sex without sobbing. There wasn't much fun to be had anymore. It was all just way too sad.

When she came wandering back from a walk on the fourth day, Roscoe pulled his car into the driveway with a wave even though he had been warned to stay away because of the flu.

Luna stopped mid-stride with her hands on her hips. "Roscoe, I know you missed us, but you've been commanded to stay away."

"Pshaw." Roscoe waved like it was nothing.

Luna cocked her head to the side. "Chickadee is going to be furious."

The screen door banged open and Chickadee's voice rang out. "Roscoe, you turn around. What if something happens to you? I can't live without you. You're the best goddamned lawyer in the world and you barely charge me a cent."

Roscoe smiled. "Well, Chickadee—" Dilly appeared on the porch. "—and Dilly—" Next Beckett stepped out. "—and Beckett, you're all here, so I figure I can be here too."

He reached in the back of his car and pulled out three shopping bags. "I brought groceries. Besides, I delivered all of Beckett's contracts. I've seen everyone on this mountain, had many, many meetings with friends and strangers. I was giving them good news of course, but I had to act all gracious while they cried and carried on happily on the front of my shirt. Beckett and Luna you should have been there to receive most of it, but I took the duty on, and now I could use a few days to rest. I thought, where better than inside the quarantine house?"

Chickadee said, "You're just an old softy here to check on Luna."

"That may be true and I brought chocolate. Also, as you remember Chickadee, I lost my dear Winnie and our little one to the Deep Flu. I'm immune and I don't want to stay away wondering."

Chickadee sighed. "I know, I know, I sat with you through it dear Roscoe. All right then, you can come in, but we're watching my shows, not your silly detective shows, my comedies. Got me?"

Roscoe smiled at Luna and laden with bags walked toward the house. As he stepped by Luna he asked, "How are you feeling?"

"Good Roscoe, I'm glad you're here."

Chapter 56

They all stayed up and watched movies late and Roscoe slept on the couch. Beckett and Luna stayed in their room the following morning, sleeping and reading and cuddling so as not to wake him up too early. Beckett got up first. "I have to go use the bathroom. I'll tell you if the coast is clear."

A few minutes later he called, "Luna, come out here. You need to see this!"

When Luna emerged there were flowers all over the living room, and Roscoe, Chickadee, and Dilly stood in the middle of them. "Ta-Dah!"

The room was beautiful. Roses, peonies, carnations, and daisies, in glass vases wrapped in brightly colored ribbons, with balloons gently bouncing and floating here and there covering every surface and the floor. Luna asked, "What is this? Did you do this Roscoe?"

Roscoe said, "Not me, these are from all the families on the mountain."

Dilly mopped her eyes.

Chickadee said, "They're thanking you, dear Luna, for keeping their children from the war, and hoping you. . ." Her voice trailed off unable to say the unsayable.

Tears welled up in Luna's eyes. "Oh, that's really wonderful. I haven't met many people yet, they're strangers, and that's just so thoughtful."

Beckett hugged her. "Quite a few of them plan to come in person to meet you too."

Dilly said, "Look at the time, I was about to come drag you out of bed, because the seamstress, Millie, will be here in a few minutes."

Luna asked, "What seamstress?"

"For your wedding dress," said Dilly. "I told her that you were quarantined and she said, 'That sweet girl will have a wedding dress. I don't care about the germs.' Said they can put the whole mountain on quarantine if they must. Besides, we all lived through it already."

"Oh, that's really—"

Chickadee held up her former wedding dress with another, "Ta-Dah!" Yards and yards of white fabric and lace and weighed down the bent hanger. Chickadee's bicep bulged with holding it. She pretended to buckle under the weight. "I floated down the aisle, didn't I, dear Dilly?"

Dilly smirked, "Like a beautiful gossamer cloud."

Chickadee chuckled. "You wrote a poem like that about me once, if I remember correctly."

Dilly gasped, "I did, I can't believe you remember my old poems!"

Chickadee laughed, "I do, remember them all." She tapped the side of her forehead. "I have a memory that holds every single line. I'm also too shy, as you know, to recite them, so you'll just have to trust me that I do."

Dilly kissed Chickadee on the cheek and then there was a knock on the door. "The seamstress!"

Chapter 57

It was hot and Luna stood for a long time. Chicka-dee's heavy wedding dress was draped all around her body, and Millie chattered constantly about what a dear she was, how she had saved the whole mountain, and touched every life. "My niece Justine was going to lose her boyfriend to that war, but he got his contract from Beckett yesterday and well, the whole family will be here, I'd say, by tomorrow to hug you themselves."

Luna was holding her arms out, her belly protruding, her shoulders shifted forward, her lower back aching. Millie poked pins through the sleeves transforming them into caps, ignoring Luna when she said, "Possibly I want a sleeveless dress, like a tank top."

"With wide shoulders like this," said Millie, "you'll want to hide them with some capped sleeves."

Luna sighed. The baby kicked. The heat sweltered. The day dragged. The flowers steamed.

While Millie was still there poking pins The neighbors from two properties over came banging onto the porch calling, "Hullo, Chickadee, Beckett!"

They were all introduced to Luna. Then each in turns held her hand, told her how much she meant to them, how much they adored her, and how grateful they were. Then right before they had left, another family, with eight

people total, knocked and entered. The round of intro-
ductions began again. Roscoe brought glasses of tea for
everyone and passing by Luna said, "Told you the grati-
tude was exhausting."

But not for long, because three minutes later Luna's
knees buckled, and she sank to the floor in a faint.

Chapter 58

Luckily Luna missed the freak out scene that followed. Beckett carried her to the bedroom, sweat rolling down his face, unable to say anything because he was insanely close to punching someone in the face. Who, it didn't matter. His fury was faceless.

Millie was in a high-pitched frantic-panic.

Dilly was buzzing around getting everyone to their feet to leave with her best wishes and thanks.

While Chickadee stood frozen in the middle of the room with Roscoe patting the back of her hand and telling her it was nothing but a thing. "Not a bit of a worry. Luna passed out. Pregnant women do that."

Chickadee said, "If something happened to that girl, it's my fault, you hear me Roscoe, my fault."

"Now, now, it's no one's fault. It's the nature of the virus that it does what it does."

Beckett lowered Luna onto their bed and dropped to his knees beside it. He brushed her hair from her forehead. "Luna? You with us?"

Dilly bustled in with a wet rag and two drops of tincture for Luna's tongue, a drop for Beckett's tongue, and one for her own. "For panic."

Beckett ignored her and kept whispering to Luna. "Luna? You here?"

Her eyes opened out of focus at first. "What happened?"

"You kind of disappeared for a minute, sank right into the pile of dress. Dilly and I had to dig you out."

"It's just hot."

Beckett searched her face. "Is that all? You're not excessively tired or weak?"

"Beckett, I'm way pregnant. Yes, I'm tired and weak." She stroked fingers along his scruffy chin and he sat looking at her face.

She asked, "What are you thinking about?"

"I'm not really thinking, I'm still trying to get my adrenaline out of my ears. I thought my head would explode when you sank down, and I had to weave through all those people to get to you. I almost knocked over Old Lady Jespen, because she wouldn't move fast enough."

"She might be like eighty."

"Yeah, yeah, whatever, I would have liked to see a bit more hustle." He gave her a sad smile.

She gently pushed with a fingertip the spot where his dimple should be. And pushed harder until he smiled.

"Thank you. We're all so damn glum."

Beckett put his head on her chest and a hand on her stomach searching around for the baby's lumpy-busyness. "Has the baby been kicking?"

"Yes, a lot. Right now. . ." She waited for a minute, then pulled his hand to her right side. "There. Baby wants to say hi."

"Hi Baby." Beckett's arms went tighter around Luna's head and around her stomach. His shoulders shook as he cried, lying on Luna, feeling his baby kick, Luna's fingers twisting through his hair, scared out of his mind that this was it, and soon not anymore.

Chapter 59

Finally day six came. It was marked with temperature readings and more worrying. The incubation period of this known virus, the Deep virus, was upon them. Beckett woke, checking inside his body for the sign of anything amiss, but he was probably immune. He had been alive fifteen years ago at the edge of his mother's bed, begging her to live through, please. He remembered how, his seven-year-old brain had wanted his mom to stay alive for a very selfish reason, to protect him from his dad. Then when his mom died, he believed his selfishness had killed her. But he couldn't dwell on that for long, because after his mom died he got his ass beat pretty regularly, supposing that his dad thought Beckett had killed his mom too, and that sucked. Until his dad died eight weeks later. And then, because Aunt Chickadee was away at college in the city, and wasn't there to protect him, his uncle had taken over Beckett's beatings.

Beckett had spent many a day wondering why he lived when his mom hadn't made it. How did he have a magical immune system? It didn't seem fair to be left alone to fend.

And Luna could leave him alone again.

But the day passed, uneventful. There were a lot of hours in a day, though. No hour was a safe hour because the next hour it might happen. Because the Deep Flu was known to hit like a freight train.

Beckett was bracing for the crash.

Also, he was pretty sure that if something happened to Luna, he would break apart. Because what would be the point — before meeting the baby? They went to bed on day six still wondering if something could happen in the night.

Chapter 60

The morning of day seven, Beckett curled into Luna's side and kissed her shoulder. She put her arm out for him to put his head on. He nestled there watching her face. Waiting.

Her breathing seemed fine. Her color was healthy. She looked the same. Besides the fainting the other day, healthy enough.

A phone was ringing in the outer rooms. Probably someone calling to check in on Luna. He had turned his own ringer off. He rolled up and glanced down at his phone on the floor beside the bed flashing with insistent notifications. Dan's name at the top. He needed to call him when he knew.

Beckett laid back down and watched Luna's face. Waiting. Why wasn't she opening her eyes? She seemed fine, but then again. . . His heartbeat raced, was she sick? He nudged her. "Luna."

She opened her eyes. "What?"

"You okay?"

"Yeah, oh Beckett, I'm sorry, I thought you knew. I was enjoying the peace of the moment, day seven, and I feel fine."

He kissed her all over her face and then for a while on her mouth. "Day seven. You feel good, not even a bit achy or a cold or anything? Could you be immune? God, this is amazing." He kissed her again. "You're immune! You think you were exposed?"

"Or the part of me that's sea god is indestructible." She grinned widely.

"Now some might say we have to count this day too. That you aren't out of the woods completely yet."

Luna kissed Beckett on the tip of the nose. "I'm calling this a win."

"Me too." He looked down at Luna's stomach, "How about you baby, win?"

A lump rolled over across Luna's belly and she giggled. "The baby agrees. Let's go do something today."

"You want to go to Heighton Port?"

"Yes!"

"Okay but first, Chickadee and Dilly are right outside the door, waiting to hear. . ."

Luna shook Beckett's head off her shoulder and bounded up. She ran across the room and threw open the door, "I'm perfect!"

Chickadee and Dilly were sitting in the living room facing the bedroom door. They jumped up at Luna's words and began to applaud. Everyone hugged all around. Chickadee mopped at her eyes. "I just—Luna—I'm speechless."

Beckett came out and hugged his Aunt Chickadee. "You're speechless? I've never seen that before."

"Well, I don't think I've ever had this hard of a week, I'm not sure what to do with myself now that I don't have this fear settled in my bones.

Dilly said, "I know what you can do, help me plan this wedding!"

Beckett said, "Luna and I can't help today. We're going to Heighton Port to spend the night with Dan and Sarah.

Dilly put her hands on her hips and pretended to look stern. "A vacation? With this much planning to do — fine." She smiled. "More for me to do, anyway."

Chickadee said, "It's your dream come true, getting to plan without any input from anyone else."

Chapter 61

Luna and Beckett held hands outside the front door and Beckett knocked loudly. Dan whipped open the door. "Army!"

Beckett hugged him. "Not army anymore."

"Sure, but it's a personality thing." Dan held him at arms length. "You can take the boy out of the army but you can't take the army out of the boy."

"I don't know, I like to think I'm evolving."

Sarah hugged Luna. "So you're all clear?"

Beckett said, "We're all clear, no flu. Luna must have picked up an immunity somewhere."

Dan said, "Plus the sea god thing."

Luna laughed. "That's what I was saying!"

They all traipsed into the kitchen and crowded in chairs around the table. Sarah said, "Next we need to say thank you. That was really so unexpected and amazing."

Beckett said, "You got your contract?"

Dan said, "We did. We haven't been able to totally wrap our minds around it. Having a baby wasn't an option for so long that we haven't started yet—"

Beckett laughed. "You only heard about it two days ago."

"I figure the sooner we start trying the better, right baby?" Dan kissed Sarah on the cheek.

"You are incorrigible." Sarah blushed. "I dumped my birth control in the trash yesterday. We are so excited. Thank you. I'm not sure how we'll ever repay you."

Luna beamed. "Have a baby, I want to be Aunt Loony."

"Alrighty then, I see we have work to do, honey want to go to the bedroom?" Everyone laughed. "Seriously though, I need to feed all these troops. What are you interested in eating and are you staying the night? And are all the plans on for the wedding? And Luna I didn't want to say this when you walked in, but are you sure you're going to have the wedding before the baby, because you look like you're going to pop."

Luna stood and turned left and right showing off her tummy. "I'm the size and shape of a buoy. My seamstress thinks she can somehow make me look svelte and beautiful in the wedding dress, but I think I'll look like a tent."

Dan looked at them both and shook his head. "But look at Army there, can't take his eyes off you. What do you think Beckett, will Luna be the prettiest three-man tent you've ever seen?"

"By far," said Beckett and pressed the back of Luna's hand to his lips.

"It's a beautiful day out, will you be paddling today, Luna?" asked Sarah.

"No, I'm hot, tired, and heavy, plus, Beckett could use the break from worrying about me. I think I'll stay on shore today."

Dan said, "What if we walked along the docks? Look at the boats? Enjoyed the beautiful day? Then we can come back and watch movies and eat."

"That would be perfect," said Luna. "Besides, Beckett needs to research the kind of boat he's going to build." She grinned at Beckett teasingly.

"Army is going to build a boat? Awesome! Can I come watch?" Dan put his chin on his hand.

Beckett laughed. "I get it, it's hard to build a boat. You don't think I'm up to the task. But I've got a tool belt, a snarky navy guy, a biologist, and a pregnant sea goddess, I'm sure we can figure it out. Unless a boat down there has a for sale sign. I'd pay big money to save me the ridicule."

After a big dinner they all, including Rebecca, took seats in the living room. The movie they were planning to watch was called, Crazy Loves, and the critics called it "true escapism for the times in a funny laugh romp of a story," which seemed perfect for the night.

The only problem was that as they switched on the television there was a flash of a news story that caused Beckett to lean forward. "Wait, what?"

The newscaster said, "...the furthermost Outpost #349..."

"Is that yours?" Dan asked.

"...has collapsed. Now the passageway from the southern point to the northern pass will be unmanageable by Nomadic Water Peoples. Their trade routes have been cut off. With the loss of this Outpost, one of the last still standing, their way of life is at risk. Director Smithsonian of the Interior Department had this to say," the video switched to an earlier recording of a doughy-faced man in a suit and tie saying, "we warned them to come to shore and offered them settlements. Our next step is to pass the bill I'm sponsoring, requiring all Nomadic Water People who continue like this to face arrest."

The reporter asked him, "Do you have the votes to pass the bill?" Director Smithsonian said, "Definitely. By the end of summer anyone still out on the seas in a man-powered watercraft will be removed from the ocean by force."

Beckett squeezed Luna's hand.

Dan gestured at the screen. "What about the floating outposts? I've seen the designs, they could implement them easily. Besides we'll all be in boats someday. We'll all need supplies. Jeez that's so shortsighted."

Beckett turned to Luna. "It's gone. Where we met, just gone."

Luna said, "Poor Sky. What are they going to do?"

They all sat quietly for a moment. Then Dan asked, "Still in the mood to watch the movie?"

Luna nodded. "Yes. I need the laugh. Especially with the storms coming."

Everyone turned to Luna.

Dan said, "The weather forecast is clear for the next two weeks."

"Did you guys not see the sky today? There will be rain starting Wednesday, and it will go for days after that."

Beckett squinted his eyes. "Our wedding day?"

Luna said, "We'll need to tell Dilly to plan it for indoors."

Beckett moaned. "I think she'd rather postpone it. She has a whole vision."

There was a collective sigh. Beckett said, "Nothing we can do right? Got to live through and laugh if we can. How about this movie, Dan?"

"What's happening — who stole Army and replaced him with Chill Dude?"

Beckett said, "Told you, evolving."

Chapter 62

Ten days later, Beckett woke up mid-morning in a room that was still darkened. "You were right, it's pouring outside." It was the day that was supposed to be their wedding day.

"I'm always right about the weather."

"Well, I'm glad we were able to postpone it, because from the sound of it there's a river running through the garden where we were planning to say our vows."

Luna hooked a hand behind her ear. "Listen, that's a waterfall through what was going to be the dance floor."

Beckett sighed."The rain, it's unrelenting."

"It's an excuse to stay in, read books, watch tv?"

"True that, but I also have chores, wet, wet, sopping, wet chores. I'll get them done fast." He lifted the blanket to climb out of bed and then climbed back under, twisted around and down so that he was eye level to Luna's tummy. "Baby, here's the thing, we've had to postpone the wedding until next Saturday. It's getting really close to your due date, but if you can you should hold on, because I'm trying to marry your mom before you're born. Okay, please?"

The baby kicked right at Beckett's nose. "See, baby understands."

Luna asked, "Why is that so important to you?"

Beckett turned to his back, one arm stretched over his head. His ear was beside her belly button. "Call me old fashioned, but we should be married before we have a baby. So the baby will have my last name."

Luna squinted her eyes. "Can't Roscoe simply handle it all anyway with the magic swirl of his lawyer pen?"

"Probably, but it's not the way it's supposed to be done. We're supposed to fall in love, get married, then have the baby. There's an order to it."

"Okay, Mr. Old Fashioned, You skipped 'have sex for the first time' should be after 'get married,' and in that case the boat has sailed." She rolled to her back spread-eagle.

Beckett admired her rounded stomach, "That's no boat, that's a ship, I mean look at it, a big ship too, like the ones that carry all the containers."

Luna giggled.

"When did you say the midwife will come?"

"You're going to pick her up the day after the wedding and she'll stay until the baby is born."

"I'll clean out the extra bedroom for her today. How old did you say she sounded?"

"I'm guessing she's a spry one hundred and three. But I might be underestimating by a few years."

Beckett groaned. "This is going to be an interesting honeymoon."

"Best part? She said she wanted to make sure she can watch the MUC channel. Because she likes to stay on top of the government's doings."

Beckett groaned louder. "The Mainland Unified Channel? It's meetings and speeches interspersed with propaganda. Chickadee is going to have a freaking fit."

"That's not the worst of it. She mentioned that she especially loves Senator Harnage."

"The architect of the Refugee Solution — yep, Chickadee will kill her. If she says one anti-nomad or refugee thing in this house, I'll have to tie Chickadee to a chair."

"She's the only midwife for miles and she's all we've got."

"That's the reason I'll tie Chickadee up."

They both lay quietly for a moment. Beckett asked, "But this is all fine, right? You've got this? I shouldn't drive you to the hospital?"

"I've got this. The hospital is full of the Deep Flu epidemic, anyway. And birth is easy, I've read the books, we've watched those terrifying videos."

Beckett jokingly shivered.

"The midwife, as old and neo-mainland, as she is, will be here, probably. . ."

Beckett jerked up his head to look at her. "Probably?"

Luna ran a finger along the edge of the sheet draped across her belly. "I have a feeling I know when the baby is coming."

"When?"

"The full moon is tomorrow."

"I didn't ask that, I asked when is the baby coming."

"And that's my answer. The night of the full moon, probably."

He furrowed his brow looking up at the ceiling. "Wait, what?"

"Because of the gravitational pull."

He rolled to his stomach and shimmied until he was eye level. "The gravitational pull?"

"And the high tides."

Beckett shook his head. "Seriously?"

"Seriously. Give or take a few days. Possibly a week." She grinned. "But definitely by the end of the month."

"Just not on our wedding day, please." He kissed the tip of her nose. "And better would be *after* the wedding, I'm just saying." He sat quietly for a moment. "Because of the tide?"

"Yes."

"So the water rising can be a good thing. That's what you're saying?"

She kissed him on the lips. "In this case, yes."

Chapter 63

Beckett woke up with a start. Luna's side of the bed as empty, a splash of moonlight pooled on the wrinkled sheet

He picked his watch up from the bedside table, two in the morning. Luna was up walking around unable to sleep but that was perfectly normal for her. Probably. He strapped the watch to his wrist and climbed out of bed, yawned, thinking if he kept his eyes closed he wouldn't wake all the way up.

He was exhausted. After the two days of rain, today had been clear, so he had spent it building the first fence. To divide his remaining land, now more like a big yard, from the government's land. The land he had given away was full of trees and fields and places he used to call his own. It was going to be a nostalgic and difficult job, not just physically, also demanding his good spirits, but the physical part was hard enough.

He had been up with the sun and collapsed at the end of the day.

Luna tried to help, but she was hot, heavy, and very tired. Understandably. Plus, it was his work to do.

He squeaked open the screen door and scanned the porch — empty.

But in a pool of light Luna was standing in the middle of the lawn. He walked down the steps, his eyes adjusting to the dim light focused on her glowing form.

She whispered as he approached, "Do you see this moon, Beckett? It's so big and beautiful it's eclipsing the whole sky. Look, you can barely see a star. It's glowing so brightly that it's darkening everything around it, taking over, but then, over there, see?" She pointed to the northwest horizon. "The bright star in that corner of the sky? That's the tip of the Monarch's wing. It's sparkling and fluttering and carrying a message across the sky."

Beckett was staring up, mesmerized, but also, frankly a little sleepy-eyed and dazed, to be standing in the heat of a summer night, staring up in the middle of the dark. "What's the message?"

She continued to stare at the sky. "Get ready, it's coming."

"What's coming?"

She turned her eyes to his face. "The baby."

"The baby? Oh, really, the baby, right now?"

Luna grinned and nodded.

"What do we do, do you need to lie down?"

"We have some time yet, can you walk with me up to the viewpoint?"

"Let me grab my phone."

He raced into the house, passing Dilly, who sleepily asked, "Is Luna okay?"

"She says the baby is coming."

Dilly squealed, "Oh, yes, oh oh oh, awesome. Where is she?"

"Outside, we're going for a walk. Back in a bit. Can you make some food, for later?"

"Definitely. Grab your phone—"

Beckett held up his phone to show her as she said it, grabbed his shotgun as a precaution, and raced by her to meet Luna.

The side of the mountain up to the viewpoint was well lit by the moon and the trail was easy to see. Luna hooked her arm around Beckett's elbow and leaned, heavy, as they walked. Mostly she was quiet, but occasionally she spoke. "Did you know that there is a snail that leaves a bioluminescent trail and sometimes that trail can still be seen days later, shimmering and. . ." Her voice trailed off. She walked quietly for a few minutes.

Beckett finally said, "I didn't know that."

She seemed to have forgotten what she had been saying and so said nothing, just quietly, heavily, walked.

They arrived at the viewpoint and Luna lowered herself to the bench.

Beckett dropped down beside her watching her face for any sign of what he should do to help.

She stared out into space.

"You doing okay?"

She nodded. "I think I need to sit and stare for a while."

"Sure. We should walk back soon though."

He watched the horizon too, but it only took a moment before his eyes closed and his head lolled as he struggled to stay awake. "Want to go back yet?"

"Not yet." Moonlight bathed her face. Her hand rubbed a circular pattern on her stomach.

"I have to — I'm going to lay here for a few moments. Promise, if I fall asleep, you'll wake me if anything happens?"

She nodded.

He leaned his gun behind the bench, laid on his side, head against her thigh, his torso so long that he had to prop his feet out to hold himself on the seat. The end of the bench jutted into his butt cheek. It was very awkward and uncomfortable, but it only took about two minutes before he was asleep.

Luna sat. And stared. And she waited.

About thirty minutes passed and Beckett's phone rang, waking him with a start. "Huh, what — hello?"

Chickadee's voice demanded, "Where are you guys? Are you going to have your baby in the goddamned woods?"

He put his hand over the receiver and looked around sleepily. "Luna, you okay?"

Luna was leaned forward. "Shhhhhhhhhhhhhhhhhhhhhhhh."

He whispered, "You okay?"

She nodded. "I'm not shushing you, just for a while this is the only thing I can do that feels okay."

"Crap, okay Chickadee we're coming back, I fell asleep—"

He hung up to Chickadee's voice yelling, "What the hell do you mean you fell asleep!"

He helped Luna up and tried to hustle back, but she needed to stop every few minutes to lean over, hands on her thighs. "Shhhhhhhhhhhh. shhhhhhhhhhhhhhhh."

The fifth time she remained bent for a long, long time. Beckett was trying to be patient, but also wanted to get her home out of the dark woods. "Ready?"

She was quiet.

He waited some more. "Ready to walk?"

She straightened. "I can breathe again, but we better walk fast."

Chickadee jumped to her feet when Beckett and Luna made it to the porch. "You're scaring the hot mess out of me. What were you—"

Luna said, "Shushshshshshhhhhhhh," and walked by focused on getting to her bedroom.

Chickadee muttered, "What in the world?"

"That's what she's been doing for an hour or so." He placed the shotgun in its rack over the door. "Dilly can you get some ice water? Luna," he called, "need anything?"

"Nothing—shhhhhhhhhhhhhhh." She disappeared into their bedroom.

Beckett ran a hand over his head. "Someone going for the midwife?"

Chickadee said, "Peter is headed over there now, but it will be six before they arrive. Tell her to hold on."

"Yeah, that might not be possible. I'll tell you if there's anything else."

Luna was sitting on the bed, leaned back on her arms, sweaty head, tousled, messy hair, sticking, wet cheeks, red flushed, shhhhhhhhhhh. The room smelled of lavender and mint, candles burned on the dresser and scents clung to the air.

Beckett closed the door and sat beside her. "How's it going?"

"Shhhhhhhhhhhh." She moaned and dropped to her knees, the top half of her body draped on the bed.

He jumped for the door and received the glass of water from Dilly and brought it to Luna. Their eyes met momentarily, but hers were unfocused and drifting. He stuffed a pillow under her knees.

She ripped her shirt off over her head, half-stood, and gestured at her legs. "Take my. . .off."

He pulled her pants down and tossed them away.

She returned to kneeling and Beckett listened. Her breathing was deep, sleep-like, the whole room still and quiet. Then she would shift, her breath would quicken, her body would tense and work and move. Her hands clutched, tugged, and stretched the sheets. And she'd moan and shhhhhhhhhhhh until slowly she'd collapse into the semiconscious half-sleep for a bit. Then the wave would begin again. Beckett listened for the shift, counted the time, found his own breath quickening with hers, as the waves came closer, steeper, and more difficult for her to ride.

After about an hour she added the word, owwwwwwwwwwwiieeeee.

Beckett asked, "Okay?"

She nodded. "Shhhhhhhhhhhhhhh."

Dilly knocked on the door. Beckett opened it a crack and she asked, "Does Luna need me?"

"Luna, do you need Dilly?"

She shook her head and moaned again.

Dilly said, "Peter called. He and the midwife are still two hours away, and traffic is terrible, could be longer.'"

Beckett scrunched up his face. "I don't think we have that long. Can you tell Peter, thanks, and to drive faster? Then call Dr Mags, tell her we're having the baby and ask her to come? She didn't think she was qualified for the birth, but it would be good for the baby, I think."

"Definitely. Anything else?"

"More ice chips?"

He closed the door and dropped to his knees beside Luna.

She gestured frantically at her lower back. Beckett gingerly stroked her skin.

"Massage my freaking fragnastic back, Beckett, freaking push on it, before I freaking go scream into the woods, goddammit, shhhhhhhhhhhhh."

Beckett massaged.

"Harder. Harder."

He pressed with as much strength as he thought she could bear, and she was still moaning. He pressed harder.

"If you don't press — shhhhhhhhh. Ow ow ow owwwwwwwwwwwwieeeee. Crap, Beckett, stinkcrawling, fudsuperlicious — shhhhhhhhhhhhhh — owwwie owiiieeeee."

Beckett massaged, watching the side of her face. Her eyes were clamped shut. "You cool?"

She gasped out, "How freaking long?"

"Um, like two hours?"

"Freaking scatrastic monsterjiminy—ooooooowwwwwwwwww, shh, owie-owie owieeeeeeeee." She moaned and dropped her forehead down to the bed panting. "Okay, that—why are you still massaging my back?"

"Um, because you told me—"

"Stop. That's over. We aren't going to do that anymore."

"Okay, good because that was—"

She raised back up on her hands. "Owwwie owwwie, freaking oh shhhhhh owie owwwwwie. Massage — now, now, now. Owwwwie, no no no nooooooooooooooooowie. Stop. Nooooo."

She collapsed onto the bed. "I don't want to anymore."

"Okay, we won't anymore. Do you want me to massage your back?"

"No." She panted and raised up on her arms. "Oh crap, oh crap, owwwwieeeeee, oh no oh no oh noooooooooooo." She dropped back down on the bed.

He stroked the wet hair off her forehead.

She said, "Okay that was the last one I'm going to do."

"That sounds good."

"I want to go do something else now."

"Like paddle, we could go to Heighton Port and paddle out for the day."

She nodded her head and laid there for a few moments panting, so quiet that it seemed like she might be asleep. Then she said, "That sounds good. This sucks I don't want to anymore."

"I agree, but you know, I think you have to if we're going to meet the baby."

She scowled and raised up. "Arrrrrrr-owwwwie owwwie owwwwwwwiiiiiiiiieeeeeeee. No no nooooooooooo."

Her sound switched suddenly to a deep guttural, "Unnnnnggggghhhh," and she didn't collapse forward but said, "The baby, the baby is—"

Beckett dropped down behind her and looked up.

"Unnnnnggghhh, the baby—"

"I see it. I see it, Luna, just—"

She grunted again and the baby's head fully emerged. "Catch the baby."

"I know, one more, okay?"

Luna raised taller and grunted, bearing down until the baby slid from her body down into Beckett's waiting hands.

Luna burst into tears.

"Can you drop back for a moment?" Beckett helped her move a leg, bringing the baby around and up in front of her.

She spoke to it. "Baby?"

The baby looked up at her and Luna started laugh-crying. Beckett started laughing too, with tears rolling down his cheeks.

They both sat and stared down at the baby. Luna asked, "Oh baby. That was really hard. Was it hard for you too?"

As if in answer the baby screwed up its face and made a small crying sound. Then it quieted again staring up into Luna's eyes.

Beckett wrapped his arms around them both. "You made a baby. You can freaking do anything."

Luna nodded. "I did, I made a whole baby."

A few minutes later she passed the baby to Beckett, had another couple of contractions, and delivered the placenta. Beckett said, "I just realized it's a boy."

"It's a boy?"

"It is. You made a whole little boy."

Luna cut the cord and Beckett tied the cord with a piece of colored string. He wrapped a sheet around Luna and the baby, forgetting that there was anyone else in the whole wide world, until they were brought back to the present by a timid knock.

Dilly asked through the door, "Beckett is everything okay? It's super quiet in there."

Beckett whispered, "You ready to meet the world, baby?"

Luna said, "We're ready."

He opened the door and whispered, "Luna had a baby."

Dilly said, "A baby?"

Chickadee came running from the front porch. "A baby? Already?"

Beckett laughed. "I don't know about already. I think that was plenty long enough."

They helped Luna up to the bed and surrounded her with pillows and towels and sheets.

Everyone gushed at the beautiful baby and beamed and exclaimed and gave blow by blow reports. Chickadee teased, "I have never once been shushed like that."

Beckett said, "You know that's bullshit."

Dilly said, "Watch your mouth in front of the baby Beckett."

Chickadee joked, "That baby has been exposed to enough bad language. We could hear Luna carrying on through the door."

Beckett asked, "Was that bad language? She kind of sounded like a toddler pirate."

Everyone laughed. Chickadee joked, "It's all fun and games now, but we're going to have to have that wedding dress altered again."

Luna groaned, and everyone laughed even more.

Finally Chickadee said, "Roscoe is here. He's been on the porch since four in the morning, waiting to hear. Can he come in?"

Luna said, "Of course."

Chickadee and Dilly left to rustle up some breakfast.

A few moments later Roscoe appeared in the doorway. "Hello Luna, Beckett, congratulations."

"Thank you, Roscoe."

"I, um, won't stay long," He tapped a large envelope on his leg. "I have a gift for you. Really it's for Luna and the baby. I would like her to have it now that the baby is safely on the mainland."

He passed the envelope to Beckett, who peeled the end open and pulled out a stack of papers. He read the top and showed it to Luna. "It says, the Last Will and Testament."

Roscoe nodded. "In it I name the baby as the beneficiary of my estate."

Luna said, "Really, Roscoe?"

"It's not as much land as you once had, but it's a working farm. In the past three years I added a lot of steer to it. And I have a few men who work it for me, so this isn't a job, it's an income."

Beckett said, "Wow Roscoe, I never imagined."

He nodded quietly. "You'll also see, once you flip through the pages, that there are seven more wills, naming your baby as heir. Families without much, but they're giving it all to you as a thank you for your kindnesses, Luna. In the end you'll have almost as much as you had before."

"Wow," Beckett said again flipping through the pages.

"You were becoming used to the idea that you wouldn't need the land or the income, Luna. It was very selfless what you did, and I am in awe of you. But I believe in the future you'll need something, land or money, so these families are providing for your son." He clapped his hands down on his knees. "I'll need to take the papers with me and continue the process. You'll let me know when you have a name picked out?"

Beckett smiled, "You'll be one of the first to hear."

"Sounds good." Roscoe left the room.

Beckett turned to Luna. "That was amazing."

She said, "I gave everything away and now my son is richer than ever. It's some strange mainland magic."

The baby closed his eyes and fell asleep in Luna's arms.

Then Beckett shifted beside Luna on the bed, an arm wrapped around her shoulders, and they all three fell asleep before breakfast could even be served.

Chapter 64

A few days later Luna stood in the middle of the floor, baby tucked in her arms, breastfeeding, while Millie, the seamstress, attempted to alter the dress once more. Everyone was there watching.

Millie jabbed pins around Luna's belly area. "It would be easier if you had the dress all the way up on your shoulders."

Luna grinned. "Baby's gotta eat. Can you put in some panels right up front, so I can just lift them to feed the baby?"

Chickadee laughed gleefully.

Millie looked shocked. "You intend to nurse the baby in the middle of your wedding ceremony?"

"Only if he's hungry. It seems like panels would be easier than lifting my skirts all the way up over my head." Luna grinned, enjoying Millie's discomfort. She had after all vetoed Luna's choices and called her shoulders 'man-like.'

Dilly tried to translate. "I think what Luna's trying to say is she'd like to conveniently feed the baby on her wedding day. Before and *after* the ceremony. I'm sure it's a rare request, but if anyone can pull if off, it would be you, Millie."

Millie pinned a fold over around Luna's puffy belly. "Well, of course I can do it, it will just require more patching."

Chickadee held up a pile of chiffon and satin. "There's still plenty of fabric, patch away!"

Beckett added his opinion. "You'll need to work on the top of the dress anyway, Luna's breasts are probably double their former size."

Millie pulled to a stop. Beckett added, "I vote for just removing the top altogether. Who's with me? Topless bride?"

Chickadee burst into laughter. Luna passed the baby to Beckett, pulled the sleeves of the dress up on her shoulders, and allowed Millie to attempt to button up the back. But there was no way to get it completely closed. Millie sighed. "Fine, we'll just start over. Panel here, panel there, no topless bride while I'm the seamstress."

Beckett and Luna met each other's eyes, and Luna giggled.

Dilly said, "All this talk of patching has me worried, please make it beautiful too."

Beckett kissed the tiny fist of the baby, watching Luna, hands out, dutifully still, while the seamstress poked pins all around her dress. "Look at her Dilly, everyone, have you ever seen anyone more beautiful?"

Luna blushed.

Dilly said, "Aw."

Chickadee said, "You are such a sweet boy and no, I've never seen anyone as beautiful. You're right."

Millie said, "I will put my heart and soul into making this dress match this beautiful girl for you."

Beckett winked at Luna with a grin.

Chapter 65

On the day of their wedding Luna woke up to Beckett's voice. "Wake up, baby, wake up." Beckett was nose to nose to the baby. He looked up into Luna's eyes and smiled. "Good morning! Today's the day. Are you ready?"

Luna smiled and rubbed the back of his head. "I am."

"No, the answer is 'I do.' We've been over this and over it. If you don't say, 'I do,' at just the right time, with just the right amount of solemnity combined with happiness, people will whisper that it's a shotgun wedding."

Luna giggled. "You see this baby? Literally everyone thinks it's a shotgun wedding."

Beckett joked, "Are you telling me you had a baby? I hadn't noticed." He kissed the baby on the nose and shimmed up to kiss Luna. He ran a hand along her stomach, tickling the lines and marks that were left behind by her pregnancy. "You were really pregnant, weren't you? That will teach me to not believe you."

"I was definitely pregnant, now I'm a mom, and I'm five hours away from being Mrs. Beckett Stanford. When you said people, you mean the twenty close friends and family, right? A modest garden wedding, like we talked about."

"You know as well as I do that the number has ballooned to astronomical proportions. Dilly is trying to

250

keep the final headcount from us so we won't panic. You, my dearest Luna, are beloved in these parts, literally *everyone* will be there."

Luna giggled. "Who would have thought giving all your stuff away would make me so popular."

"Our stuff, you literally gave away all of our stuff. You're a nut job." He pushed a dark curl off her cheek and tucked it behind her ear.

"I'm your nut job, Nut Job Stanford." She kissed him sweetly. He ran a hand through her hair and kissed her again.

"Speaking of names, what are we going to name baby? I'm leaning toward — I don't know. I thought Dylan was good yesterday, but now I'm not so sure. Maybe we should consider your Dad's name?"

"It seems like an old guy name, not a baby name. I can't decide."

"We're thinking about it too hard. It will come to us if we take it one step at a time. First, I give you my last name, then we give the baby a first name, and then we legally give the baby my surname, and it will go perfectly with the first name because it is. . .?" Beckett gestured for Luna to say the first name that popped into her head.

"I got nothing, except Sugarbunny. Sugarbunny Stanford?"

"I love you. I suppose I should go help the crew with the preparations."

Chapter 66

Chairs filled the garden. Luna counted ten across and but stopped counting at five rows back and refused to do the multiplication because she didn't want to know. Her job was to sit in a chair and nurse the baby. Which she did happily because the preparations were hectic and outrageously detailed. Some guy that was there helping mistakenly asked her where a bouquet were supposed to go and she said, "Um, the table?" He huffed and disappeared to ask Dilly. Which was just as well, Luna didn't care where the flowers were, but Dilly was enjoying every second of planning and organizing and decoration.

At last it was time to get a shower and hair done and dressed while Beckett helped with all the other things. They were not supposed to see each other the day of the wedding, for some reason. Everyone seemed to have ignored the morning waking up together — that didn't count.

And this didn't count — when Luna was in their bedroom gathering her things for a shower. There was a knock at the window and Beckett grinning through the screen. "Chickadee told me she would make me sit in a time-out if I came to see you, so since I could use a break I figured seeing you was a win-win." His grin widened. "You getting naked for the shower, can I watch?"

"Okay, first, if it's bad luck to see the bride on the day of the wedding, one hundred percent it's bad luck to see her naked. That probably brings earth shaking calamity, and we've literally had enough of those."

"True that, but not anymore, now it's happiness from here on—"

"Beckett! You're going to jinx us. I love you. You happy? You healthy? Our baby perfect? Our neck of the woods in order? Yes. Let's accept the perfect present of this day."

"God, I love you, can I come in, just for a few minutes? You're about to be naked and—"

"That's the second thing, Beckett, I have just had a baby. I am still bloated, oozing, covered in stretch marks, purple lines, have you seen my thighs, because I haven't, and I'm wondering if this might be it, my permanent shape from now on — if you go on and on about how sexy I am, I'll think you're not to be trusted."

Beckett clutched the windowsill and sighed dramatically. "Fine, send me away, but I might be so distracted by longing that I'll forget my wedding vows."

Luna's eyes grew wide. "Beckett, I am counting on you to be the cool civilized one that knows everything so I can forget what I'm saying and stutter and — promise me you remember your lines. Promise."

"I do. See, that's all you have to say. Oops, I think I hear Chickadee, I better run." He disappeared at a jog around the house leaving Luna giggling in their room. She tucked the sleeping baby, surrounded by pillows, in the wide middle of the bed, gathered her underwear and brushes and combs and lotions and oils and headed into the bathroom for a shower.

Later she was standing in their room again, Sarah putting the finishing touches on her makeup, while Luna watched their reflection in a long mirror leaning on the wall.

Dilly was buttoning the back of the wedding dress. Millie had done an excellent job, but in the past few days Luna's breast size had gone down, and her belly had gotten a bit smaller. Dilly said, "Hold the flowers right here, so no one will notice."

Chickadee stood beaming beside her. "Dearest Luna, you are beautiful. The white looks stunning with your dark hair, just exquisite."

"I've never worn white before. I think I'm going to get it dirty."

Chickadee humphed. "Well, of course you're going to get it dirty. On my wedding day I myself got a chocolate cake smear right on the ass, and not one person said anything, because I looked so spectacular it didn't matter."

Dilly added, "That being said, learn from Chickadee's mistakes and use a napkin when you eat dear, and it will be fine. And we aren't worried about anyone else wearing this dress because no one else in the world would have your particular shape." She and Chickadee giggled merrily.

Then Chickadee fussed with the veil and the flowered headdress and became serious. "I want you to know dear Luna that I love you. You are the best thing that ever happened to the boy, and he knows it to his core. I always believed he deserved better than he was given, and here you are. You hold that head up. Ignore the hundred and twenty or so people who are—"

Dilly said, "Closer to two hundred. We had to make the buffet potluck because so many people wanted to come."

254

Chickadee continued, "It doesn't matter how many, ignore them. Aim for Beckett. His smile at the end of the aisle. That's all you have to do and a few minutes later you're officially a part of my family, and I can dote on you properly. Isn't that right, Dilly?"

Dilly sniffled and nodded. "I have a present for you." She pulled a small jewelry box out from under the makeup kit. "This belonged to my grandmother, passed to me, and now you. It was true what I said in the beginning, that even if you and Beckett didn't have a happily ever after, you would still have a home. I meant it, because you've so perfectly fit our family. I can't think of anyone better suited to wear these." She thrust the clamshell shaped silver box into Luna's hands.

Luna was surprised and teary-eyed. She fumbled with the clasp until the box flipped open — a beautiful necklace, three strands of pearls with a diamond clasp. Luna said, "Oh my. For me? I've never had jewelry before."

"Yes, you. It will be beautiful with your dress. Plus pearls come from the sea, so it's fitting." She settled the pearls around Luna's neck, resting on her collarbone, and fastened the strands in the back. She and Chickadee in unison clapped their hands. "Perfect!"

"Really?" Luna's dress was formfitting white satin. The skirt sank to the floor and swished and floated with a bit of chiffon underneath. At the top there was a low plunge of cleavage, small button folds for breastfeeding access, and the capped sleeves that Millie insisted on.

Chickadee and Dilly both said, "Really," and then as if a spell was broken they both at the same time said, "So much to do."

Chickadee said, "I'll go make sure all the guests are seated and that Beckett is in place."

Dilly said, "I'm going to spin the area and make sure everything is done. We're leaving you with Sarah for a few minutes, and then I'll come get you and the baby, okay?"

They spun out of the room and away.

Sarah said, "This is a wonderful family you have."

"I feel so lucky that I found them through Beckett, and he's the greatest."

Sarah nodded. "You're pretty awesome too." She fluffed up the bottom of the skirt so that it floated perfectly. "I ought to go now to my seat. Dan and Rebecca and I are in the front row. Don't be nervous. This is supposed to be fun, and when it gets scary, remember that Beckett is at the end of the aisle."

"Aunt Chickadee said that too."

Sarah smiled. "Great minds think alike."

"Speaking of great minds, did you make a baby yet?"

Sarah sighed. "Dan has put his heart and soul to the project and is barely letting me do anything else. We'll see. I should know by the end of the week."

Luna grinned. "Please tell us as soon as you know."

"Of course, and I'll see you on the other side." Sarah left to go join the audience.

Luna stood in the middle of the room. She had wondered if her mind would be full of worries and logical impediments to a seafaring-girl marrying a land-based boy, but happily her mind was full of one thing — that first night they were together when he tied the pretend knot for her before they
fell asleep.

He had smiled at her that night, making the knot-tying unnecessary. The smile alone was enough for her to follow him anywhere, and then happily, luckily, gratefully, he was so much more. She giggled at the memory of him calling, Anna! And jumping from the boat. That had been a truly spectacular belly flop.

A few minutes later Dilly ran back in, the music following her. "Ready?"

Luna picked up her sweetly sleeping baby. "Ready."

Chapter 67

The side lawn of the house had been mowed. The chairs stood in rows and were completely filled. People milled around the edges, standing without seats, a few people thick in places. So many. Many, many people. Luna in her whole entire life had counted her family and friends on her fingers and toes. Crowds were rare until she came on land.

There had been islands and Outposts and port landings with crowds of people, but she had been a visitor, a passing-through person. Now she was a living-here person and these people all had heard of her, were here to see her. They wanted to meet her and speak to her. It was terrifying actually.

She gulped and followed Dilly out the door, across the porch, and down the steps to the grass. Dilly stopped and turned to adjust her veil and headdress. She told her one more time that she was beautiful. "Okay follow me to the beginning of the aisle and you'll go down it by yourself."

Luna's eyes went wide. "By myself?" There had been much discussion about the day but that part hadn't completely sunk in. She repeated, "By myself," passing the baby into Dilly's arms.

Dilly led Luna to the aisle and as Luna's eyes scanned the crowd, faces turned toward her, people stood to get a better view, gaping and gawking. It made Luna a little dizzy truthfully, the sea of faces all watching her walk. Dilly kissed her on the cheek. "Eyes on Beckett." She left for her seat.

Beckett.

Beckett was waiting at the far end of the aisle, wearing a dark suit with a light shirt and looking so handsome. He grinned happily with a full dimple showing.

She wished she could return it, but her shoe had caught on the back of her veil with a tug and the whole headdress slid off the back of her head to the ground. She turned to grab it before it hit the dirt, but missed, and there it was, dirty. Plus, the turn threw her a little off balance, and balance hadn't been easy for a months and months. She was out of practice. Her arms careened to hold her up, but she wondered if she might fall down again, into her dress, or better yet, more grown up — pull the skirt up over her head and hide there until this storm blew over.

"Luna," Beckett waved his arms, "wait there, I'm coming for you!"

She nodded her head gratefully.

Then Beckett did this — he pantomimed diving into the middle aisle. Grinning, he stroked toward her as if he was swimming.

Luna cocked her head to the side. "Whatcha doing Beckett?"

"Swimming to you, of course." He switched to the backstroke, then the breast stroke. He pretend to come up for a breath and a look-around, checking to see if he was off-course.

Luna giggled.

He stroked again, until he stopped in front of her, pretending to tread water. He held out his hand. "Can you swim?" He sounded a lot like that first night on the Outpost, *can you dance?* It made her knees kind of weak.

She took his hand. "Have you met me? I'm half mermaid."

He side-stroked through the air up the aisle with Luna a step behind pretending to breaststroke.

The entire audience was laughing by the time they made it to the front. Luna pulled beside Beckett, where she had been told to stand, and they held hands and waited for the ceremony to begin.

The minister, an old family friend, had a smile on his face. His part of the ceremony was long. Later, everyone said it was beautiful. The words spun around Luna, words like heaven and earth and all the spaces between, filling her with happiness, though later she couldn't recall any of them. Simply, Beckett and Luna, and then Beckettand-Luna together, and finally the minister said, "I believe Luna has something she wants to say to Beckett." He closed his book and waited expectantly.

Luna and Beckett turned to each other holding hands. She stared up into his eyes.

She had suddenly forgotten all that she wanted to say, so she improvised. "We made it."

Beckett said, "We did. We are."

She looked down at their clasped hands searching for the right words and looked back up into his eyes. "When I first met you I believed you were afraid of the world. But in mere days I knew you were the bravest person I have ever met."

Beckett chuckled, "I don't know, I've had a mild sense of panic over you the whole time we've been together."

Luna shook her head. "Well, it doesn't show. What shows is from that first night when you wanted to make me feel safe before I fell asleep. The day you leapt heroically from the boat to swim to me. When you battled the storm to rescue me—"

Beckett interrupted, "I don't think that's how it exactly happened."

"It's exactly how I remember it, and my memory is perfect. And that's what I wanted to say, but it's hard to find the words — meeting you on the Outpost was like finding my perfect other half. Like coming home. The Monarch Constellation is touching the Breeze Constellation, and it's brought disruptions, but together we can navigate them and find our way home together. Because you're my home. My everything."

Beckett nodded. "Thank you Luna."

The minister said, "Beckett would you like to say something now?"

"I would." He looked down at Luna. "Remember that first night we were together?"

Luna giggled. "The night we made our baby?"

Chickadee in the front row cackled so loudly that people all through the audience started laughing too and everyone had to wait for the audience to calm down. When order was restored Beckett joked, "What — we made a baby?"

The audience laughed more, for longer. Luna gestured toward the baby in Dilly's arms in the front row, and Beckett acted like he was only just now seeing it. He shook his head. "I mean, I'm happy, but I wish you would have told me."

The laughter finally died down. Chickadee was mopping her eyes with a handkerchief, sitting between Roscoe and Dilly, leaning between the two to say, "That girl, I do love her."

Beckett said, "So it's safe to say you do remember that first night."

"I do."

Beckett grinned. "Now see that was a perfect, I do. It's just not the right time."

He took her hands and enfolded them in his, pulling her a step closer, and looking so deeply into her eyes that the whole world fell away. Suddenly it was just the two of them, alone, like on the Outpost. He paused long, staring into her eyes.

She felt a tremble to his hands. Her heart filled with so much love for him that she felt breathless, overcome.

He smiled a half-smile and speaking only to her, said, "The sun was setting. You had just read me some Calvin and Hobbes comics. And you pretended to love what I cooked." He let go of one of her hands and pushed a lock behind her ear, letting his fingers touch her cheek overly long.

His voice was low and tremulous, the kind of voice that would break with emotion, but couldn't because what it wanted to say was so important, had to be said. "You told me that if I watched the sunset and really concentrated, that at the moment the sun sank behind the horizon, there would be a flash of light, and in that flash would be the instructions for the whole wide world."

Luna pressed her cheek to his fingers. "I remember, and you didn't see the flash, so—"

"I lied." He said it like an exhale.

Luna raised her brow. "You lied?"

"I did. I saw the flash, and I received the instructions. I just didn't want you to know because they were all about you."

262

Luna was mesmerized and weak-kneed, barely able to gasp, "And they were?"

Beckett strengthened his hold on her hands. "One, you love her. Two, she gives you hope. Three, don't ever lose her."

"And you haven't."

"I thought I did, but I found you, and I keep finding you, and I won't ever stop."

Tears welled up in her eyes. "Thank you."

He placed his hand behind her neck and pulled her forward and spoke in her ear. "No, thank you. For it all, for everything — for saving my life."

That was it, she was crying. Her arms went up around his neck and she clung to his chest, his arms around.

Beckett whispered, "Can we keep going?"

She shook her head, crying into his jacket.

The minister asked, "Do you, Luna Saturniidae, take Beckett Stanford to be your lawful husband?"

She sniffled and her muffled voice came from inside his hug. "I do."

Beckett whispered into her ear, "Perfect."

The minister asked Beckett if he took Luna to be his wife and he answered, "I do." Then Beckett pulled two rings from his pocket and fumbling, put one on Luna's hand, and she put one on his.

The minister said, "You may kiss the bride."

Beckett's hand trembled as he lifted her chin, and met her lips in a kiss that tasted of salty tears, but was also deep as their feelings, and as fresh as their hope. Because marriage was for their future, their family, and meant that there would be a tomorrow and a tomorrow after that, and they would meet it together.

Dan clapped loudly. "Bravo!" Shaking them from their private moment.

Beckett and Luna turned to the audience, clasped hands, and stepped into the cheering crowd.

The end*

---

*Unless you'd like to know what they named the baby, then read on.

What They Named the Baby

A bit later, Luna was sitting in a rocking chair on the edge of the lawn, nursing the baby, watching Beckett dance with Aunt Dilly in the middle of the grass, along with most of their friends and family and the surrounding community. The tempo was upbeat, so Luna had decided to sit this one out.

But the next song began slowly and sounded familiar. Beckett came to her chair and put out his hand. "Would you two like to dance?"

Luna took his hand and let him pull her and the baby to the dance floor. He wrapped her in an arm and began to sway, holding them both.

"Is this the song from the Outpost?"

"It is." Beckett hummed in her ear. "I'd spin you, but there will be no baby dropping tonight."

They swayed and cuddled and hummed under a sky flung with stars.

Finally Beckett said, "I want to talk to you about something. There's a word I thought of, it means beginnings and possibilities, all the best things begin with it — like you, like the baby. It's dawning on me that it would be a really great name."

"What is it?"

"Splash."

"That's perfect. Splash Stanford. I love it. You're going to make me cry again."

Beckett swept out an arm. "How can you cry under a
beautiful night sky like this, at the end of a perfect day, a
sleeping baby in your arms?"

"It was perfect wasn't it?"

"It truly is."

And that my lovelies, was Luna's Story.

Also by Diana Knightley

Leveling: Book One of Luna's Story

Under: Book Two of Luna's Story

Deep: Book Three of Luna's Story

Check DianaKnightley.com for new releases.

Acknowledgments

Thank you to Isobel Dowdee for being my story editor, advisor, and for loving the story. I'm sorry it made you cry. Your thoughts and ideas made it better and better.

And thank you to Kevin for being my resident paddleboarding advisor. Watching you paddle from Catalina to Manhattan Beach inspired me to create this whole world.

And to my kids, for giving me the space and time and love to finish these labors of love.

And thank you to my mother, Mary Jane Knight Cushman, she was a hopeful soul and taught me if the waters rise to grab a paddle.

And finally, to my father, Dave Cushman, who taught me that any story, like life, is better with a punchline.

About me, Diana Knightley

I live in Los Angeles where we have a lot of apocalyptic tendencies that we overcome by wishful thinking. Also great beaches. I maintain a lot of people in a small house, too many pets, and a to-do list that is longer than it should be, because my main rule is: Art, play, fun, before housework. My kids say I am a cool mom because I try to be kind. I'm married to a guy who is like a water god, he surfs, he paddle boards, he built a boat. I'm a huge fan.

I write about heroes and tragedies and magical whisperings and always forever happily ever afters. I love that scene where the two are desperate to be together but can't because of war or apocalyptic-stuff or (scientifically sound!) time-jumping and he is begging the universe with a plead in his heart and she is distraught (yet still strong) and somehow, through kisses and steamy more and hope and heaps and piles of true love, they manage to come out on the other side.

I like a man in a kilt, especially if he looks like a Hemsworth, doesn't matter, Liam or Chris.

My couples so far include Beckett and Luna (from the trilogy, Luna's Story). Who battle their fear to find each other during an apocalypse of rising waters. And, coming soon, Colin and Kaitlyn (from the series Kaitlyn and the

Highlander). Who find themselves traveling through time and space to be together.

I write under two pen names, this one here, Diana Knightley, and another one, H. D. Knightley, where I write books for Young Adults. (They are still romantic and fun and sometimes steamy though, because love is grand at any age.)

13107923R00162

Made in the
USA
Monee, IL